Soulpushers
By Lola Lariscy

Acknowledgements

Thank you to B.B. who helped me get this book in motion!
Also thank you to John Ward for the great cover art and to Kelly
Smith for formatting so professionally.

Thank you to Dayline (D.J.) Jusino for translating the bits of Puerto
Rican Spanish.

Prologue

The woman watched as David kicked the ball around the field. She could almost see her child's shadow. She knew she was being foolish. Souls didn't have shadows. There was no outward appearance of her daughter.

Would she have liked soccer? She had always pictured her daughter as a ballerina, but maybe she would have liked karate. Or paintball. Or band. Maybe she would have liked them all and she'd have spent thousands of dollars and hundreds of hours on after-school activities.

She clamped her smile down before it had a chance to form. She'd never know what her daughter liked. She was lying in a bed in the back of the family house. Comatose, but not medically so. Physically, she was fine. Her heart beat, her blood flowed, and her brain sparked. No regular doctor would ever determine why her daughter had never woken up...why her eyes had never opened on their own, or her voice had never made the tiniest sound.

The mother didn't want to go home. She wanted to hide behind that tree forever, watching her daughter's keeper play ball. Looking for any sign of her daughter's personality. But she couldn't. The coach called for the kids to leave the field, and the other mother rushed up to claim her son.

Zoe and David

"Shut up. Why do you want to tease me all the time?"

Because it's easy. Because you're a captive audience. It's my way of punishing you for being free.

David kicked a pinecone along the worn-out path. They'd been through that park hundreds of times, and they'd had similar conversations hundreds of times. He knew she didn't mean it. She wasn't being malicious—she was just bored and trapped. He'd probably feel the same way.

"Alright," he responded. "Keep antagonizing me. But my taste in music is *my* taste in music. I let you listen to that Swedish pop music. Do *not* give me grief for listening to 70's funk. I'm trying to grow my repertoire—move beyond what's on the top ten list."

He sensed her frowning. He needed her to know he was serious. He took out the music player and found the first file with a Swedish title. He hovered over the "delete" button.

Okay! You've got me. I won't laugh every time you play some grand funk junk. Truth is, I like it, too. It's just so much fun to get a rise out of you.

"Yeah, whatever," he said, as he kicked the pine comb farther down the path.

———— • —— • ————

David checked the mail on the hallway table before going up to his room. Another flier advertising half off oil changes. He wished they wouldn't address mail to the Byres family. How did they know there was a family? He could be one sad, lonely man waiting for a letter from a daughter who never wrote. He could be an orphaned child staying with distant relatives who were biding their time until he was old enough to leave.

Eh, he knew he was being overly dramatic. He was David Byres, son of Alan and Mercedes Byres. The fact that Alan Byres no longer lived in the house didn't make his upbringing any less tolerable. Nothing in his life was worthy of a TV movie...well, except for one part of his life.

The weirdest thing in his life was Zoe. Well, *she* wasn't the weird part. He rephrased the sentence in his head. *The weirdest thing is that Zoe is stuck with me.*

Thinking of Zoe, he went back to scanning the mail. He was looking for a letter from the science institute. That would be for Zoe—science was her thing. He liked music and soccer.

He heard a noise. He looked up from the mail and caught his mother's reflection in the mirror. Moments like these he saw how much he looked like her. Growing up, he'd cringed anytime an aunt or grandmother had remarked on their similarity. However, standing there—he aged 16, she aged 40—he had to admit that her mocha coloring, wavy brown hair, and dark eyes were his, too. She was a child of Puerto Rico. By extension he was, too. Maybe if his dad came to visit, he'd have similar feelings toward him, and toward Ohio.

The sweet, reflective moment ended. His mother narrowed her eyes, and David immediately tensed.

"Do you have practice tonight?" she asked, approaching the table, and taking the mail out of his hands.

He nodded, as he did every Tuesday night.

Her gaze narrowed more. "But not here."

This wasn't a question—more of a directive.

He sighed and nodded, as he had every Tuesday night since the drum kit incident. One broken window...one angry neighbor...one police vehicle and the fun was ruined for everyone.

David started up the stairs, assuming the ritualistic grilling was complete. But his mom wasn't done. She tilted her head, as if that would help her see her son better. "You know, David...I love you, and I support your decisions. I just don't understand them. Why science camp? My sister tried to talk to you about her work in neurology, but you pretended to be ill. What's going on?"

She held up a pamphlet for Johns Hopkins University. "Why are you interested in this?"

He shook his head and ran up the steps so fast he almost fell forward. He landed squarely on his bed. "Why do I want to go to Johns Hopkins?" he asked out loud.

You don't, dweeb. I do.

He groaned. He didn't feel like having this conversation again. "Yes, but I'm the one who has to apply. I'm the one who has to tour the college...go to class."

Yeah, but you get the parties, the late-night burritos, the... She faltered, unable to think of a third perk. Instead, she changed the subject. *Your mom reminded me that I'm mad at you. Why wouldn't you talk to your aunt when she came to dinner?*

David set his phone alarm for an hour. "We've been down this road before. I would have had to pause for you to say the question and then ask the question out loud. You know how odd that makes me sound."

David fell asleep, but Zoe stayed awake, counting academic degrees like some people counted sheep.

—— • —— • ——

Herb liked to be called Herb, though his name wasn't Herb. He shed his first name, Andrew, as soon as the school bell rang.

He was the new image of an old concept: the quintessential jazz musician, with his old-fashioned name, thrift store clothes and blustery saxophone. His eyes squinted and his cheeks reddened with the effort of producing the wan notes that rippled through the family room. One four-minute solo would blow out all of his energy. Halfway through the evening he'd fall onto the couch and pass out. Thus the "Herb break" was born—five minutes of guitar, bass and drum riffing by David and the other bandmates.

Zoe piped up, too—though since no one but David could hear her, they still needed a corporeal backup singer. That position was filled by Herb's sister Renna.

———— ● —— ● ————

Herb and David had bonded immediately back in the fifth grade. Herb had caught David shouting at a wall. Since kids were staring, Herb had started answering "What?" like David was talking to him. He hadn't known why the boy was yelling at himself, but it wasn't any stranger than Herb telling his sax to simmer down because the sound was just too sweet to handle.

There hadn't been a connection so strong since Lennon and McCartney, Simon and Garfunkel, or Sun Ra and the planet Saturn. This was what Herb wrote in his memoir-in-progress, anyway.

David didn't consider their meeting so historically significant—more personally significant. He'd finally learned to get out of his own head and interact with the human race. Or, at least a few select representatives.

Science Camp

David and Zoe had hit on a compromise. The only science that held David's interest was geology. He actually liked learning about igneous rocks and strata. Unfortunately, there weren't a lot of large rock formations in Florida. So, after some research (which unfortunately David had to stay awake for, since he still officially controlled the typing), they hit upon a science program at a university in Georgia. It was a practical program that didn't involve research, so David liked that aspect of it. The program lasted 2 weeks, and it hit on most disciplines, which Zoe liked. Most importantly, the school's geology program sponsored a field trip to a local mineral-rich natural landmark.

David's mom didn't like the idea of putting her son on a bus to an unknown land, but she also didn't like the idea of driving him 6 hours, just to drive back. She considered asking his dad to deposit him, since he was stationed almost halfway between. She didn't, though. She'd already asked more from him than she wanted. Plus, she didn't think David would go along with the idea.

In the end, she agreed with the bus idea. Within two years he'd be on his own for real, and now was a good time to get a little practice in. Besides, she'd been put on a plane, on her own, to Puerto Rico when she was eight. David was twice that age. He'd be fine.

———— • ———— • ————

The ride up I-75 was placid for David, mainly because he'd slept most of the trip. He'd learned early on to sleep with his eyes at half-mast so that Zoe could look out if she wanted or needed to. This had probably cost him a few friends and acquaintances at sleepovers. There is a certain level of creepiness to a sleeping person looking awake.

The science program provided a private bus from Atlanta to the school. The Jacksonville kids' excitement drummed up as they boarded with kids from other points around the Southeast.

The bus rambled along. The kids' excitement boiled over as their phone apps lit up with notifications that they were approaching...stores that were all available in Jacksonville or wherever each kid was from.

Sadly, the bus driver wouldn't stop. Plenty of kids tried. David noticed one kid with buzz-cut sandy blond hair get out of his seat and approach the driver. He froze when the driver glared at him in the rear-view mirror and backtracked to his seat.

They turned onto a local road. Pretty soon they approached a group of traditional red brick buildings. They were all very serious buildings. He didn't feel like a serious person.

The kids, aged 13 to 17, were limited to a small area of the school—basically the dormitories. Stepping outside of the bounds was forbidden, except when going with the group to class.

The unofficial first day challenge was to rummage around the abandoned dormitories, looking for brag-worthy pieces of contraband. David didn't participate because he didn't really want to be there. His body was there, but his mind was in his room, picking out guitar chords. Of course, they hadn't let him bring his guitar. The admissions person had let David's mom know that it was because they didn't want to be responsible for stolen items. She also admitted that the head of the program didn't want all night jam sessions. Apparently that had happened.

Zoe didn't want him to do anything that could get them kicked out, so he was happy to stay in the dorm and think of lyrics. So far, they hadn't taken away his small notebook and pen.

After a while, he decided to go downstairs and see what kind of books they had. Despite not being a "science guy," he was impressed with the dorm collection. Books on computer science, physics, neurobiology, and other fields that David had barely heard of. He noticed a pamphlet for an institute of robotics. Apparently, it was possible to earn a master's degree in the subject.

He heard a soft weeping. He realized it was internal, so he sat down, trying to steady himself.

"Are you crying?" he asked Zoe.

Next came a soft gulp from deep within his mind.

No. I'm not crying. I'm dying. Can we please go to college here?

"Probably not. How about let's just enjoy the two weeks we have here."

They heard a noise from the hallway outside. The boy from the bus—the one who almost caused them to wreck by trying to get the driver's attention—ran into the library and dove onto one of the sofas. He looked around nervously.

"Did anyone follow me?" he asked.

David narrowed his eyes. "No. We've only been here two hours. Who do you expect would follow you?"

The kid grinned and raised up onto his elbow. He used his other hand to remove a small device from his pocket. David didn't know what it was, but it looked like contraband.

"What is that?"

"This," he said, dramatically flourishing the device, "is what our parents used to put addresses in."

"Huh?"

The boy rolled his eyes. "It's a PDA," he said, huffing.

"A PDF?"

"No..." he drew out, slowly. "It's an old-style electronic organizer. It's like a dummy smartphone."

"Huh?"

"Except it doesn't make calls."

"Could I type in it?"

"Yeah, I guess. I mean, that's pretty much all it does, besides calculating."

"Can I have it?" David asked, thinking about how much he hated physically writing.

The guy shrank back, horrified. "Back off, man! This is mine! Go steal your own archaic device."

David decided it wasn't worth discussing. The little pen thing looked annoying, anyway.

———— • ——— • ————

The kid's name was Dempsey Roslo. He'd become sort of famous in the day they'd been there. No one else had found anything noteworthy, so the new challenge had become to steal the device from him. Not easy to do since he brought it into the bathroom with him.

Dempsey was glad the bathroom wasn't communal, like his mom had said she'd had in college. Her dormitory bathroom had had a line of bathtubs separated only by shower curtains. In this set-up, he only had to share the bathroom with one other person, and that person wasn't set to arrive until the next day.

He spent that whole first day trying to get the device to work. It had been dead since probably before he was born. Yet, within two days, he had it humming. Well, as much as a dummy device with a 16 MHz processor could hum.

The Wi-Fi in the dorm had been shut off because the kids were supposed to be learning the old-fashioned way. Their minds were supposed to be focused on the practical application of science, not on homemade explosion videos (not that the personal digital assistant could play those).

Dempsey had other plans, though. He remembered that the university had a huge computer lab that would probably be open during the summer. Day two saw him sneaking off to the lab. Access was free, and shopping was abundant. His folks had given him a credit card to use for emergencies.

He knew just the site to go to for the items he needed. His only problem was how to receive them. Kids also weren't allowed to get packages, especially packages from online retail stores. So, Dempsey waited for his unofficial muse, Opportunity.

Opportunity came in the form of a scraggly, disheveled summer student. Dempsey saw him through the window, across a small grassy area, near the library. The student paced back and forth, shouting words that were inaudible, and probably not allowed in Dempsey's household. The guy was pressing the power button on his phone tightly. As hard as he pressed the phone, though, nothing worked. The phone was dead.

Dempsey, sensing a common purpose, approached him with a deal. Within two business days, the guy had a new battery (courtesy of Mr. and Mrs. Roslo) and Dempsey had what he needed.

His last order of business in the computer lab was research. He found dozens of practical jokes, none of which seemed *too* risky. He spent an hour typing out instructions and formulas into the PDA. It took him a while to get used to the pen that had come with the personal digital assistant. The student had been the one to tell him the pen was called a "stylus." It didn't seem very stylish to him.

David was trying to like science camp. He was trying to make friends. The chemistry kids always smelled like, well, chemicals, and they spent all their time in the lab. The physics kids were out of the question; they were always talking about stuff way over his head. He couldn't tell if Zoe understood them. She would never admit if she didn't.

He eventually settled in with the geology kids. Seismic shifts and volcanic activity began to fascinate him. He had always thought of the ground as being one of the few stabilizing factors in life. Finding out that wasn't true didn't upset him, though. Instead, he was excited that there were things he still didn't know about his surroundings. Maybe he could strike a deal with Zo and major in geology.

On the first Saturday of camp, the geo kids went to the fault. David was surprised to see Dempsey Roslo on the bus with them. He didn't think Dempsey had any interest in anything but tech and engineering. He'd skipped most of the classes in the morning, though geology was afternoon.

The bus wound through miles of rocky terrain and forested landscapes. David had copied some puzzles and logic games using the library's copier and was *trying* to work on one, but the clucking in his head was getting in the way of concentration. Clucking was the sound Zoe made when she was thinking deeply, but still wanted to get his attention.

What? he thought.

Dempsey, she thought back. *He wasn't around at all last night. That kid makes me nervous. He's up to something. Would you go talk to him?*

"Oh freaking hell," David said, under his breath.

———— • ———— • ————

Dempsey was at the back of the bus. Not surprisingly, he was alone. David stumbled down the aisle and fell into the seat next to him. Walking while in motion was not one of David's strong suits.

"I'm surprised to see you here. I was starting to think you'd come to this camp for the fish sticks. What made you decide to come with us?"

Dempsey put away his archaic device. David didn't understand what he saw in that thing. It didn't even play music.

"I got called into the admin office yesterday. If I want my credit, I have to go to every class and outing. Tonight, I'm stargazing off the highway. I don't even like astronomy. I want to be a magician. Engineering will help me with that."

"Don't you think physics would help you, too?"

Dempsey considered this and nodded his head slightly. "Maybe. But I've pretty much learned everything I need to know online, anyway."

David frowned. He didn't know much about physics, but he knew that it was more complicated than a video or forum could teach.

———— • ———— • ————

The bus pulled up to the park gates an hour later. David hoped these geology kids accepted him after this. Otherwise, he would've just stayed back at the dorm and slept.

They took the tour: plate tectonic forces, hanging walls, subduction zones, etc. etc. David thought he heard Zoe snoring. Finally, they were herded out to the open, where the grand remnants of millions of years past were laid-bare for all to visit.

David had a pretty jaded view of anything touristy. He rolled his eyes at the RVs lining the parking lot and he laughed at the trinkets sold in the shop. He wasn't rolling his eyes or laughing when they got to the fault. He'd never seen anything so raw and beautiful in his life. A huge chunk of land had shifted up, above the plank of land they were standing on. Patterns he'd never seen in nature covered the surface of the rock. Each layer had a story. He realized he had no idea what those stories were, though. He *was* a terrible science student.

He looked around for the professor, but saw Dempsey instead. Dempsey wasn't looking at the fault. Instead, he was looking nervously off to the side, into the woods.

David looked around some more. He still didn't really know these kids. He barely knew their names. There was one girl he thought was interesting. Her name was Yvonne. He'd never talked to her, but he'd overheard her telling some of the other kids that she did biology videos. He wanted to talk to her about how she made them—for his music, not for any personal reason, of course.

Zoe brain-punched him. *Ok, mostly not for personal reasons,* he thought. He admitted to himself and to Zo that he thought Yvonne was pretty. The way the sun illuminated her dense red hair reminded him of a single rose in a garden of green. Not that her skin was green or anything. The green was the foliage around her. Zoe brain-punched him again.

They weren't allowed to touch the rock, but Yvonne was pressing her luck. Just as her arm reached out to touch a smooth swath, she started shaking.

She was knocked to the ground, just as a rumbling noise started farther down the rock face. David didn't feel anything himself, but he watched a few of the other kids slide around, and that made him feel like the ground was shifting beneath him. The other kids were covering their ears due to the deafening sound.

Park rangers arrived and began pulling the kids away from the rock face. Once everyone was a few feet away, two of the park employees went back to the area of disturbance. That's when Zoe realized that the small area was very rectangular; not what one would expect from a natural occurrence.

That's also when David realized that the rumbling noise had stopped abruptly. All he heard were squealing tires and a highly revved engine.

Zoe growled to get his attention. The rangers had dug into the ground with two small shovels and excavated two long contraptions. They were two mechanical earthquake simulators. Someone must have come in early and set it up. Why, neither Zoe nor David had any idea.

———— • ——— • ————

True to his word, Dempsey was in chemistry class Monday morning. Zoe felt David's heart sink when he realized that Dempsey was with Yvonne, huddled over an assignment. Yvonne's partner had recently come down with a stomach bug, so Dempsey was probably taking his place.

That made Zoe suspicious. All of the students had been at the same locations. Yet, no one else had fallen ill. Dempsey had known he'd need a chem partner. Had he rigged the circumstances, so he'd be Yvonne's partner?

No, she thought. She was being way too paranoid. However, she noticed things David didn't see. He was constantly distracted by outside stimuli. Zoe wasn't. Zoe could hide quietly and observe.

———— • ——— • ————

Giving half these kids access to chemicals seemed like an incident in the making to Zoe, but at least the teacher was taking them outside. More room for flames to be controlled. Or *more room for flames to expand,* she thought, pessimistically.

Zoe wasn't an expert on people-herding, but she noticed one member of the chemistry flock wasn't following the expected path.

Yvonne veered away from her own partner and settled into step with David. She leaned into him, her red hair almost brushing up against his shoulder.

"So, what are we doing, exactly?" she asked.

David, surprised, almost dropped his equipment. Zoe smiled her phantom smile. *He thought she meant something else.*

"What?" he stuttered, trying to steady the box. He cringed as each glass settled.

"I meant what are we doing today? I saw bleach on the teacher's desk."

"Oh, yeah. Of course, that's what you meant! Yeah, we're doing potassium chlorate today."

"I figured it was something like that—I overheard the teacher. We're going one team at a time."

"That doesn't seem fair," David answered. "The later teams get to watch the earlier teams perform the experiment. They get to see it done several times, whereas the first team doesn't get that."

She shrugged. "Sucks to be first!"

———— • ———— • ————

Yvonne ate those words as she was called first to the picnic table. Dempsey looked ecstatic. He was already getting the beakers out before he got to the table.

She heated up the burner and then poured in the bleach. The sun was scorching overhead, so David couldn't see much of what was going on. *So much for having an advantage,* he thought.

Yvonne filtered out the sodium chloride, keeping the sodium chlorate, which would need to cool. The teacher pointed to an already-cooled version he had prepared earlier.

Yvonne went onto the next step, reaching for the potassium chloride and mixing it in with water.

While everyone's attention was on Yvonne, Zoe placed her focus squarely on Dempsey. She didn't trust him, and he'd been way too excited about a simple chemistry experiment. Giddy was the word for him.

All eyes were on Yvonne as she mixed the sodium chlorate in with the potassium chloride, thus creating the potassium chlorate.

Zoe wished David were wearing sunglasses. The brightness from the sky washed out most of the detail. She could see a few things clearly, though: Dempsey raising his hand out of his pocket...Dempsey holding a small bag...

Zoe yelled (as much as she could) to get David's attention. He zeroed in on Dempsey just as he flicked something into the compound.

The audience recoiled in shock as purple flames erupted from the mixture. Most of the students instinctively turned away, shielding themselves.

In that moment, though, something else happened. Zoe looked through David's eyes straight at Dempsey and Yvonne. They both looked back through David's eyes, straight at her.

Zoe could distinguish, through the raw fear and confusion, these two people's auras as they turned burning-red. As she connected with these souls, she felt herself push away from David. She felt herself form the power to push these souls where they needed to go. It was like two pieces of a puzzle finally clicking together, after years of just grazing by.

Zoe also recognized something else in that moment. It was not time for these two souls to go. She pushed them back in, and as the connection broke, her tether to David brought her back down into her holding cell.

Zoe settled back down into her cubby hole. She stayed there quietly for the remainder of the commotion. She didn't want to think about what had just happened.

———— • ———— • ————

David didn't have a cubby hole. He was left staring at these two people's petrified, ashen faces. He slumped down to the ground. The chemistry teacher had recovered his wits enough to start extinguishing the fire.

Back to School

School started as it had each fall for the past 10 years. David got new clothes, new school supplies and a new headache from Zoe. Her number one thought was about who their teachers would be. He didn't care whether they got first period chemistry with the good teacher, or the third period stinker with Mr. Nathan who fell asleep at his desk, leaving the kids to spit in the Petri dishes.

He didn't even want to take chemistry...not after what happened with Yvonne. Word was that she had finished school early and headed off to college. Sounded like she had gotten the better end of the deal. She got to bypass the blandness and tediousness of high school. Also, she didn't have another soul in her body, so she had that going for her.

Wherever Dempsey was, David hoped he wasn't planning any more pranks.

David sat in the back row of European History. Any class involving memorization was a napping class. His consciousness would fade into dreams of all-night movie marathons or chords that he couldn't get just right. During those hours, Zoe took over. She was like a computer when it came to remembering names, dates, formulas, grading scales, schedules, or even grocery lists.

He was starting to nod off when he saw a familiar tangle of long, black hair hurrying through the door. As usual, he had to squint to see the skinny legs and torso underneath.

Renna looked up, smiled, and headed back toward David. He smiled too, straightening up.

Guess you'll miss your afternoon nap, Zoe thought.

He grimaced. *There's still calculus, hot shot.*

Renna pushed her hair out of her face as she sat down. David was startled at how much she was beginning to look like a younger version of her grandmother, whom he had met when they were kids. He hadn't noticed before, because she usually wore a hoodie, or a hat of some kind.

In the full light of a high school classroom, though, he could see just how much she favored her. The Native American heritage gave Renna her red undertones, and her hair—though fuller and wavier than her grandmother's—was still a rich, dark color. Her mother's African heritage was still evident, but it deepened the reddish hues from her father's side. In contrast, poor Herb was just red. He perpetually looked like he'd been left outside to bake.

David realized he'd been staring, but Renna was still smiling. He hadn't freaked her out too badly. Zoe was tsk tsking in his head, like a chiding librarian. David ignored Zoe and smiled back at Renna. Somehow, he doubted he'd learn any history.

Listen to the Band

Herb's birthday (and Christmas) present had been subscriptions to professional video software applications. His plan was to make professional music videos. It wasn't enough for an indie band member to have one talent. He had to work on the promotion, too.

His first attempt wouldn't win any video music awards. He'd spliced old footage of the band members with psychedelic pictures of herbs and flowers. He was going for a subliminal, trippy look, but it looked more like someone's attempt at a desktop slideshow.

Their band was named Herbology MindWork. He—and everyone else in the band—hated that name, but it was the only name that didn't already come up in an internet search.

They already had a hundred followers on the video channel Herb had created. Some were friends and family, but some were complete strangers who either liked the music, liked the visuals, or liked to laugh at them. Herb was fine with any and all of those.

The most impressive of Herb's marketing accomplishments had been the line of messenger bags he'd designed and ordered. The bags were durable and, well, memorable. The material was charcoal-colored canvas and each one was covered by an imprint of Herb's silhouetted head and signature curly hair.

Technically, David was the "front man," since he sang and played guitar. However, everyone knew that Herb was the star. When he wasn't hitting his sax, he was hamming it up on the stage, goading the invisible audience, and flirting with future groupies.

The bass player, Reinhard Kirby, shrugged it off. He'd be going to college hundreds of miles away and didn't much care what happened at the moment. If he found a new band, great. If not, then it meant less time in front of the camera and more time playing video games.

The drummer, Nisha Albone, didn't care who did the interviews, or even if there were any interviews. She just wanted to bang her kit. Her parents were glad she had somewhere else to play. She would've taken her drum kit out to the woods if she had to—she loved playing that much.

Renna provided back-up vocals and the goofiest dancing any of them had ever seen. Herb wasn't sure if she was hopping, dancing, or riding an invisible pogo stick. He hoped she didn't crash into any walls, instruments, or people. She was enthusiastic, though, and that's what they needed.

They loved their instruments, they loved the music, but sometimes the band members forgot they weren't alone in their rooms. Well, all except Herb. Herb always knew there was an audience.

Herb also knew they needed exposure. Playing to Herb's parents would only get them so far. With that in mind, he decided to enter them into a nationwide contest sponsored by an online video channel. Their advantages included: Herb's ambition, the band members' skills, their forgiving families, access to equipment, software, and the internet.

Their disadvantage was being one entry out of thousands. They knew there was no guarantee they'd win, but if they could just get into the finals, that would win them visibility. Maybe their followers would go up. Maybe someone besides Herb would buy a messenger bag. Maybe a record label would notice...

———— • ———— • ————

Herb had decided they needed to re-think their video shoot. Beaches, clubs, mansions, and city streets had all been overused. Barns were grossly underused.

It wasn't really a barn—it was a covered picnic area. Herb liked that the natural light came through, while still having that rustic appearance. He didn't want a modern look, so he'd asked the band members to wear loose, simple clothing. He left out the part where he wanted it to look like a creepy old-world carnival.

Herb was setting the scene up. He'd removed most of the picnic tables but had left one on each side. He planned on getting shots of tall, elongated shadows for that Dracula vibe. Because every music video that featured acrobats needed at least one creepy horror scene.

Yes, acrobats. He hadn't told them about that yet. He'd bought six green gymnastic mats. When his bandmates asked what they were for, he made an excuse about using them as green screens. That was partly true.

He took a few minutes to place the mats on and around one of the tables.

He tried to put their minds at ease by being the first. He hopped on the table and did a handstand. He choked out a request for David to start recording.

David knew what he was going for but didn't see any possible way Herb could play his saxophone while still holding himself up. David looked over at Renna. She shrugged and went over to hold Herb's legs up. David brought him the sax, and tried to hold on to him, too.

It wasn't what Herb had envisioned, but he managed to hold the sax with one hand, while the other arm struggled to hold the rest of his weight. He couldn't really *play* the sax, so much as blow at it.

The other members took turns doing somersaults across the tables. David marveled at how the shadows from the light rolled across with them. After Herb called for a break, David sat on a bench and drank some water. Zoe was quiet, no doubt mad that they weren't studying.

Renna came over and sat next to him. He liked what she'd done with her hair—It was woven into a wreath of flowers. David liked the effect—It made her look like a goddess.

She smiled and lightly punched him on the shoulder.

"You know he remembers."

He groaned, expelling air out so heavily that he choked. "It's been six years since I've been on a mat."

She kept smiling, but now a little bit of condescension had crept in. "Still, he remembers."

"That's probably why he cooked this whole thing up."

David got up and ran to the field to practice. If he was going to do flips, he needed to warm up.

———— • ———— • ————

Luckily Herb wasn't expecting Olympic-quality gymnastics, because David had never had that level of skill. Best Herb could hope for was David not splintering the wooden table. Herb pinned a silly green joker's hat on his head, and David flipped back and forth on the table a few times.

"That's it," David said, jumping down from the table. "I don't care if you don't have all the angles. Make do with what you have."

"If we don't win the video contest, it's on you."

"I doubt this would make a lot of difference," David answered, sitting on the table.

David looked over at Renna. She was sitting on the other table, waiting for Herb to call her to action. She was wearing a belly dancing costume her cousin had let her borrow. The band members were a mishmash of styles and cultures, but Herb wasn't going for authenticity. He was going for effect.

Mr. Byres

There wasn't much privacy in David's house unless he was in his own room. The living room, dining area and kitchen were all one open area on the first floor. On this particular Sunday he didn't feel like being closed off in his bedroom, so he sat at the dining room table reading history chapters on his tablet computer. He needed the distraction, so he actually read the chapters himself, instead of dozing off while Zoe took over.

He could hear his mother in the garage clearing out boxes. She hadn't said so, but he suspected she was making space for a second car. He'd gotten his driver's license, but he certainly didn't have any extra money.

After an hour of banging around the garage, Mrs. Byres came back into the house. David laughed because she had oil smudges on her face. He went into the kitchen to get some paper towels.

She looked down at the dirt on her hands and then looked at the clean table. She shrugged. She could clean the table again later. She took the wet paper towels her son handed her and wiped off her face and hands best she could.

"David, I'd like you to sit down. I'd like to talk to you about something."

David didn't like the sound of that. The last time he'd heard that tone and those words was when she'd told him his father was taking an extended work trip and didn't know when he'd be back. That had been six years prior.

They both sat at the table. His mother grabbed his hand. David became more nervous.

"I heard from your dad."

David already didn't like it. Nothing that man could say would make it okay. Nothing would make up for abandoning them.

She continued. "He wired some money for a car. It was only about $5,000, but it should be enough for a good down payment on a used car. I figured we could start looking next weekend. What do you think?"

He stared at her. "Is that supposed to make up for him exiting our lives? No 'Goodbye, Mercedes. Goodbye, David, I won't be coming back.'"

She looked sad. "Sadie. He used to always call me Sadie."

David got quiet. He could still hear Zoe's ghost breaths. *Damn, it has been a long time,* Zoe thought. *I'd totally forgotten that.*

Me too, David thought.

Mrs. Byres spoke again. This time, even more hesitantly. "David, I love you with all my heart. I've tried really hard to make a good life for you."

David was alarmed. This wasn't sounding good. Was she leaving, too?

She realized the effect her words were having. She reached out to grab his hand. "No! Everything's fine. I'm not going anywhere. I just want you to understand it hasn't been easy for any of us. I don't hold any grudges against your father. Neither of us realized when we got married how we would react to life's challenges. I became stronger during each catastrophe, and your father...well, your father didn't know how to cope. He *did* love us; he just didn't know what to do with us. I don't blame him. I feel bad for him."

"Anyway," she continued, "I think you should accept the money. He's trying to be a father—just not in the most ideal way."

David sat quietly for a minute. He knew why his dad had left, but he wanted his mom to say it.

"He left because of me."

She looked horrified and rose out of her chair. "No, David. Not at all! He left because he didn't know how to be a father. He didn't know how to behave with us, how to take care of us."

He looked down. "He left because I was talking to myself."

Mercedes sat back down. That had been a difficult time in all their lives—one she didn't want to revisit.

"Papi, none of us understood what you were doing, but we loved you. We helped you as best we could. We thought maybe it was because you were an only child. You made up a playmate, which was fine. A lot of children do that."

He cackled cynically. "Yeah, it's okay when you're six, but less okay when you're ten."

"Sweetie, that's not what I meant. We just didn't know what to do. We took you to doctors, but they just put you on medication. You needed more than that. The counselor didn't *know* why you were talking to an imaginary girl in your head."

She stopped abruptly. She was sounding more accusatory than she'd intended. She just wanted David to know that she'd loved him despite the challenges, and his father had, too.

David sat still as an owl. He didn't need to be reminded of that time. He'd learned the hard way to keep Zoe to himself. Zoe had also learned not to let herself be known. Used to be, she'd freely take over during math class, but the other kids had started to notice the two personalities. David was the slacker kid who didn't care much about school, but he was also the eager whiz kid who sat in the front row.

A ball came over the dining area. Neither felt like they'd accomplished what they'd meant to. Right then the phone rang, though, and reminded them how little time they had.

———— • ———— • ————

The hospital was bright and large. David had only been there a few times before, and each time he would have been lost, if not for his mother (and Zoe). When he was younger, his favorite spot was the gift shop, because it was close to the exit, and there were toys.

Now, though, he understood that a hospital was more than a large casing for a tiny toy store. They were there because someone dear to him was sick.

Mercedes had remained close to her mother-in-law, despite the departure of their common bond. The elder Mrs. Byres did not blame Sadie or David for her son's behavior. She'd lived with him long enough to understand where the behavior had come from.

Her husband hadn't been much different. He had been cold to both of them, and stern. She should have left him—she realized that as she had gotten older. It had seemed impossible as a young mother, though. Back then she didn't think she could support her son by herself. She'd told herself that they depended on her husband. She'd told herself a lot of things.

Now that Alzheimer's had entered her life, she didn't talk about those conflicts. Mercedes knew, though. Ada Byres had told her about a lot during those warm evenings on her porch.

When she'd first shown signs of the illness, Mercedes had arranged for her to come down South. She did fine for a few years, but within the past year she'd started slipping. Mercedes found pills that had dropped into the sheets, while there was still medicine in the pill holder that should have been taken. Mercedes would come over to find the door unlocked. The neighbors would call to let her know that Mrs. Byres was knocking on their doors asking if they'd seen her car—the car that had been sold years before in Ohio.

Mercedes had entered her mother-in-law into long-term care. It had been the hardest decision she'd ever made. Harder than even having to look for a psychiatrist for her son. Despite her son's troubling behavior, his life wasn't on the line. Ada, though, was close to her end.

Mercedes sat on the bed next to her surrogate mother. She watched her eyelashes ruffle as she took shallow breaths. She watched her hand on her chest twitch.

Mercedes sat like that for hours. David sat in the chair, next to his mother, and fell asleep.

Zoe was awake. She couldn't see, because David had his eyes closed, but she could sense. She felt a soul start to separate from its coil. She felt it coming toward her like a ship to a beacon.

The force of energy between Zoe and the soul became so strong that it jolted David awake. He opened his eyes in time to see a blinding light rise from his grandmother's body. He couldn't be sure, but he thought he saw his grandmother's face outlined in the sharp brightness.

He shook his mother awake. She yawned, but then gasped when she saw it, too. She turned to David and screamed as a trail of red light extracted itself from her son. The white light from the hospital bed pushed toward the red. The red, having softened to a haze, rose as if to greet the soul, but instead charged forward, bunting it up toward the ceiling, out of the room.

Mercedes continued to stare, shocked, well after the event had passed. Somehow her mind understood that one of the most important persons in her life had been escorted to Heaven, albeit in a way more reminiscent of a baseball game than a gentle journey.

———— • ———— • ————

The nurse stood just outside the door, careful not to make noise or cast any shadows. She didn't want any of the family to know she was there.

She hardly believed what she was seeing. Neither the woman nor the young man were Soulpushers. Yet something manifested from that boy, and that something acted very much like a Soulpusher.

She turned away. She'd have to tell the Council.

A Mental Sock on the Door

The text message came while David and Zoe were online shopping for cars. Herb was calling them back for an emergency band meeting—no instruments required. That meant business, which meant there would be tension.

They welcomed the interruption, though, having reached an impasse regarding automobile decisions. Zoe wanted a speed demon, and David wanted to keep his body intact. After all, he reminded her, she wouldn't benefit from his body being dead.

On the bus, Zoe looked down at David sifting through his text messages. He'd been sorting through the same messages for ten minutes. Surprisingly, they didn't change.

The only new text in there is from Herb about this meeting. There's nothing from Renna, despite the three texts you sent her.

He sighed. *I don't know why I suddenly care. I'll see her in a few minutes.*

Zoe became quiet. She was contemplating something—David could tell.

What, he asked her.

She took her time responding. She was obviously thinking through her words. *Have you ever thought about what it'll be like for us when we're older?*

David feigned a little more naivety. *What do you mean?*

I mean me...in your head. It'll be weird, won't it? What if you want to get busy?

He smirked, though it looked more like indigestion. *Since when do you say "get busy"? I don't know. We'll figure it out as we go along. Maybe I can hang a mental sock on the door.*

Well, what if I want to get busy?

He cringed. *Oh God. Why did you have to put that image into my head? I don't need to see you getting busy. Especially not from your perspective.*

Exactly. Now you know how I feel. I don't want to see you getting busy with anyone, either.

Zoe didn't say anything for a few minutes. The bus rattled along as the dimming sun stretched through the windows onto David's lap.

I stayed silent for eight years, she continued. *Do you remember the day I spoke up?*

Yes, of course, he responded. He remembered very well—watching cartoons one Saturday morning. The show had a character named Zoe. He remembered because an equally cartoonish voice kept repeating the name in his head. *Zoe...Zoe...Zoe...*her first utterance had been to claim the name Zoe.

That was his introduction to the oddest hitchhiker he'd ever known.

Parshall

Parshall stood outside the gates of the old Arlington mansion. It was larger and more formal than she'd imagined the Council building being. She didn't know much about Jacksonville history, but she got the sense the building dated back to the era when Arlington was considered a Hollywood of the East—back to the silent film days.

She looked down the street. There was a mom 'n pop type breakfast shop on the corner. She imagined it was the type of place where Council deals went down, between sips of black coffee and bites of egg sandwiches. She looked the other way, toward the opposite corner. A gentleman's establishment. She figured at least a few deals went down there, though probably only some involved the Council. She wondered if Soulpushers were ever called out there. Old men in strip clubs probably died, too.

She'd never met the Council members—never wanted to. She was happy being a Soulpushering cog in the Soulpushering machine. Thanks to her mom, though, the honor would be hers shortly.

Protocol was for a Soulpusher to report any unusual activity to their handler. The handler would push the info up the chain. Parshall's handler was her mom, which in hindsight wasn't the best idea. Lots of room for bickering and bruised feelings.

Mrs. Cope didn't want to be Messenger of the Crazy, so that's how Parshall ended up on that doorstep.

She knocked and after a few minutes the front door opened, seemingly by itself. There were no ghosts in the living room, so she figured the door must be controlled remotely.

The Council building felt hollow. She'd been dealing with death her whole life, but this was different. Spirits were alive to her. This house felt stagnant—vacant.

The house wasn't literally vacant, though. The front room had items in the shape of a sofa, chairs and a table. Like a cordoned off museum exhibit that had been abandoned years earlier. Dust dulled the red surface of the sofa, darkening what was probably a velvet cover.

Does anyone live here? she thought.

As if on cue, a woman about her mother's age came into the room and gestured for her to sit down. Parshall looked down hesitantly at the musty couch, but decided it was not the time to be precious about her recently dry-cleaned skirt. She wished she'd known she was going to the House of the Unclean—she would have worn her yoga pants.

After several minutes of awkward silence, the woman began staring hard at her. The kind of staring she'd only seen in movies, right before the assassin goes in for the kill.

Parshall shifted in her seat, causing a patch of dust to dislodge. The woman was still staring. Parshall didn't know what to do.

The woman set her mouth into a line that, though not a smile, at least wasn't so horizontal. "My name's Laura Altmeyer. I went to school with your mother. C'mon. I'll give you the dollar tour. It used to be a quarter, but—you know—property taxes went up."

Parshall hesitated, a little thrown off by the property tax discussion, but she followed the woman anyway. Hesitating wouldn't get her out any faster.

There was a tall, thin table standing in the entrance way to the next room. At first Parshall thought there was an urn sitting on top, but then she realized it was a tip jar. She looked at the woman.

"Really?"

The woman raised her eyebrows. "Tell ya what. Next meeting, I'll vote to raise dues. Sound good?"

After paying the toll, she followed Laura to a room deep into the house. There weren't any windows, and the only doors were the entrance and an exit across the room. The space was completely devoid of external light, but Laura flipped a switch that turned on enough wattage to light up a baseball field.

Maps and charts of Jacksonville covered each wall. Every neighborhood, including her own, was represented. Every water inlet was documented. Each patch of forest. Each road, paved or not.

"This room looks like a taxi station. Why do you have so many maps?"

She'd hit a nerve. The woman's face went back to pinched. When she spoke, her voice was clipped, sharp. "Someone has to pick up the slack. That means I have to be able to send someone out at a moment's notice to get the rogue deaths. We can't all be lucky enough to work our cover job in our reaping area."

Parshall sharpened her expression a bit, too. She hated the word reaping. It was so crass. "It's not easy being responsible for the whole hospital. If someone dies off my shift, I have to make up a reason for being there. I can't pretend to be visiting a family member, because HR knows who my family members are. I have to pretend to have left my ID, or my coat. The security guards think I'm the most forgetful person in the world."

Laura didn't seem impressed, which ticked Parshall off more.

Parshall continued her list. "Try being responsible for two souls at one time. The deaths happened at opposite ends of the hospital. By the time I got to the second soul, he was floating up to the ceiling like a balloon. It was so undignified."

The woman sighed. "Yeah, well, we all have it rough. I brought you to this room because it's secure. No one outside can see or hear us. Now, tell me what you saw."

Parshall explained sensing the other Soulpusher in the hospital room.

"How old was the kid?"

"About sixteen. But I don't think he was the pusher. I felt someone else."

"Did you recognize the kid? Is he from around here?"

"I don't know him, but I'd been talking to the mom earlier and she'd said they'd been home five minutes earlier. For them to get there that quickly, they must live close to the neighborhood."

"What's the kid's name?"

"David Byres."

Laura thought for a moment. "I think I know what's going on, but I need to look at some records. You ever want to know more about what we do here?"

Parshall shook her head before she'd even processed the question.

"Well, c'mon anyway."

Orlando

"You are not going to Medieval Times."

"Why not? How often do we go to Orlando?"

His mom stopped chopping vegetables for a moment. "We? I'm not going. I told you I have to work. You're going over to the Sheardons' tomorrow after school. Speaking of...have you packed?"

He shook his head, embarrassed that he'd referred to himself as "we."

"Alright, don't worry about helping me with dinner. Go upstairs and get your stuff ready. You're going to be gone most of the weekend."

———— • —— • ————

The Sheardons had gone all out. They'd rented an SUV so huge that it almost rivaled the SUV limos for when a politician or a famous athlete was in town. He looked for the mini bar, but Herb's parents had been proactive. All liquor had been requisitioned for the adults later.

He got in the back and was surprised when Renna climbed in next to him. He'd assumed she'd be sitting with her family.

"It's going to be a three-hour ride," she said. "It's bad enough being stuck in a room with them. I do not want to be stuck beside them in a narrow vehicle."

Nice save, Zoe thought. *You know she wanted to sit next to you, though.*

"Shut up," David whispered.

"Huh?"

David's face turned the color of the no-smoking sign. "Uh...sorry. I was talking to myself. I was going to say that I'm glad you sat next to me, but then I stopped myself because you already know."

That was either really romantic or really dumb. David wasn't sure which. She smiled, though, so it couldn't have been that bad.

"Are you nervous about being onstage?" he asked her.

"Oh! I thought you knew. I'm not going onstage. I'm coordinating the trip and acting as manager. I'm the one who reserved this vehicle, though dad had to pick it up and pay for it. But I figured it'd be good experience for me. I'm considering going to school for music management. This will be a good way to see if I really like it."

"You could manage me."

David felt a jolt. Zoe had managed to kick him from within his own head.

———— • ———— • ————

The Convention Center wasn't a center at all. It was a hub of buildings. A veritable campus that rivaled the school in Georgia David and Zoe had been to.

Renna got her first hard lesson regarding trip planning. Their event was to be held in the South Concourse. She had booked a hotel on the opposite side, not realizing that the campus was huge. So, after they checked into the hotel and decided to go to the venue, they had to contend with a small commute, hampered by a lot of traffic.

The small commute resulted in 30 minutes stuck on the thoroughfare. It seemed like everyone in Florida was trying to get to one of the buildings laid out around them.

Herb relished the captive audience. He told stories that couldn't possibly be true, not for a 16-year-old, anyway. Herb's father was in the driver's seat, and David couldn't gauge his expression from the back of the van.

David looked over at Renna. She was dozing off. He looked over at Nisha. He had expected the drummer to at least be quietly banging her knees, but she was relaxed, listening to whatever came through her headphones. The only people actually listening to Herb was Herb and *maybe* the bass player, who in true bass player form was wearing dark sunglasses.

David was thirsty, and bored. He didn't know how long it would take to get a mile down the street, but he saw a convenience store and decided he'd rather walk the rest of the way than stay cooped up in the same position.

"Mr. Sheardon," he called out to Herb's dad. "I see the building from here. Is it okay if Herb and I get out and walk? I feel like we've spent half the day back here."

Herb's father grunted. "Stay on the sidewalk where I can see you."

———— • ——— • ————

Herb and David started walking down the sidewalk. They slurped their frozen drinks and pulled strands of sour gelatinous candy apart, sucking the pieces up like spaghetti strands. Even walking slowly, they eventually left the van behind.

"So what are you going to do if we win?" David asked.

Herb kept munching, not bothering to swallow before garbling his answer. "I dunno. I guess buy better equipment. Probably try to find a publicity company. Maybe do a small tour. What do you think?"

"Sounds good to me, as long as the tour is during the summer."

———— • ——— • ————

The South Concourse was larger than their high school, and surprisingly hollow. Where most buildings would be compartmentalized into small rooms, the room they walked into was like a warehouse. In this case, though, the inventory was made up of people, booths, instruments and backdrops.

Each act had a 20 x 20 soundproofed area to show their videos, set up listening stations, sell merchandise and answer questions. The people streaming through would be an anonymous mixture of judges and general attendees. The band members had no way of knowing who held their fates in their hands. So, it was pragmatic to be polite and attentive to everyone.

They also had a choice as to whether to be "on" the entire time or relax and be themselves. Wordlessly, they all took the latter option. Even Herb chose to forgo the theatrics. There was no competing with the mess of humanity vying for attention that day. They all chose to let their performance speak for itself.

———— • ——— • ————

After the preliminary judging Friday evening (informally known as the first culling), the top 10 would get the opportunity to play live the next night. This would factor into the band's Best Performance and Best Overall Presentation scores. This was informally known as the second culling, though the results wouldn't be announced until the next day.

Sunday afternoon the bands, their families and whoever else had tickets, would file into one of the conference halls for the awards ceremony, or as it was nicknamed, the "Day of Reckoning."

———— • ——— • ————

There was very little to capture Zoe's attention, so she spent most of the first day napping. She liked music, but she wasn't exactly free to roam around. The music production demonstration sounded interesting, and she thought about suggesting it, but this was his weekend. If he wanted to go, he would. He spent an entire two weeks at science camp for her; this was the least she could do for him.

There had been another reason she'd spent most of the afternoon in a deep sleep. The moments she'd spent awake, she'd been thinking about her future. Or, rather, her lack thereof. She didn't want to spend the rest of her life as a passenger, particularly on a train she wasn't keen to be on.

Zoe had never told David this, but her thoughts were naturally shielded from him. Conversely, he had no way of hiding his thoughts from her. She was aware of every stray observation and fleeting wish, unless she was asleep. She'd never had the heart to tell him how uneven their relationship was. Her rationale was that she was protecting him, but some days she wondered if she was just lying to him.

A loud commotion interrupted her internal crisis. Not a peaceful moment to oneself in this place. The crowd was rushing from all sides to the large projected screen on the far wall. David, Renna and the rest of the entourage moved closer, too.

They were announcing the top 10. Zoe couldn't help but feel a strong sense of pride for David. This would be a big moment for him. Even if they didn't win, this was his first taste of competition. He'd either learn to face disappointment with dignity or success with grace. Whichever one, it would be a life lesson.

And the moment called for grace...David's band was among the 10. They scored well in all categories, not just one or two like some of the acts. That alone showed Zoe they had an edge over everyone else and, therefore, the best chance for Overall Presentation.

Mr. Sheardon hugged his son and daughter, while David grabbed Reinhard and they both bear-hugged Nisha, who was grinning more than any of them had ever seen.

Zoe was satisfied with celebrating on the inside, and then going back to sleep.

———— • ———— • ————

The concert started at 6 PM Saturday and each band would get 10 minutes with little time in between for set-up. The sound checks had been done earlier and each band had left their larger instruments backstage.

Zoe was so glad the band had nixed Herb's idea of wearing matching outfits. Mr. Sheardon had gently reminded him that while he dressed like he was in the 70's, most of the audience hadn't been born at that time. So instead, they all wore new, clean jeans along with simple, solidly colored shirts. So instead they looked like an ad for a clothing store.

Herbology MindWorks played third, which meant that while the previous bands played, they sat in a waiting area behind the stage. She recounted formulas in her head while the others ate candy and watched TV.

When they were called to the stage, though, she woke up. There was such a stark contrast between the brightly lit green room and the dark hazy atmosphere of the performance hall. She couldn't help but respond to the flashing lights and the cheering crowd.

The event coordinators had gone to great lengths to make it feel like the type of concert an established touring band would have. From the amount of noise, Zoe could tell the space was huge. It probably seated several hundred people and was filled to capacity. The Sheardons were in reserved seats toward the front.

In addition to hearing David's thoughts, Zoe could sense his moods. This was something she'd never felt before: Contentment. Like he was in his perfect place.

The excitement and energy were palpable. Herb was killing it on his sax. David was loving every moment on his guitar. Nisha was crashing her drums like she never had. Even Reinhard, who never seemed to care much about anything, was focused on his bass. He wasn't smiling like the rest of the band, but Zoe could tell he wasn't bored, either. He wasn't waiting for the next moment, or the next opportunity.

She looked out at the crowd. These kids had never heard of this band, never seen them play or heard their music, but they were excited, all the same. Zoe didn't know much about life, but she figured this must be the best part of it. The sense of discovery.

There was no way she was letting David live any part of his life for her. He was going to college for music, not science.

Crap, she thought. *Where does that leave me?*

The next day—Sunday—saw a lot of families in the hotel lobby. Some hadn't made it past Friday's culling, but had their hotel rooms for the whole weekend so stayed anyway. Some had amusement park badges around their necks.

David and Renna gravitated toward each other at the breakfast set-up. Renna, being mature beyond her years, went straight for the coffee and bagels. David's choice was cereal. Not the healthy kind, either. All marshmallows & food dye. Maybe he could refine his tastes by hanging around her.

The Albones—Nisha's family—turned out to be the most fun of the batch. Mr. Sheardon nearly choked on his waffles, listening to Mr. Albone talk about moving to Gainesville from New Jersey in the 80's. "The hair..." he said. "The biggest adjustment was the hair. Just as tall as New Jersey hair, but twice as wide, thanks to the humidity."

David smiled politely, but his nerve endings were on fire. All he could think about was Renna sitting beside him. He'd look over and catch her smiling at something Nisha had said or picking the bagel apart to dunk pieces into her coffee.

When David wasn't thinking about Renna, his mind seized on the ceremony. Would they win Best Overall? Would they win anything?

He came back to the conversation just in time to hear Mrs. Albone inviting them all to Gainesville the next weekend for a cookout. He could already hear his mother muttering to herself in Spanish. She thought he didn't understand, because he barely had command of the English language. What his mom didn't know was that he had a live-in language expert.

———— • ———— • ————

David looked around the theater and noted that most of the attendees looked like they were dressed for New Years Eve. Herb wore gold corduroy jeans and a gold corduroy vest over a pale-yellow satin long-sleeved shirt.

Renna wore a flowing pale-blue floral blouse with a blue skirt and dress sandals. She explained that with it being Florida, sandals were always acceptable. Nisha wore black slacks, a black satin button down shirt and Doc Martens. Reinhard wore the same clothes he'd worn the night before, hopefully cleaned. David wore khakis and a white button-down shirt. He called it timeless. Zoe called it an employee uniform.

They were all seated in the left section, 5th row, with the band grouped together close to the aisle—easier for them to get up and go to the stage if they won.

With no snacks or drinks to keep them occupied, all the kids could do was look around excitedly and tap their hands nervously on the back of chairs. The bands in front and behind them did the same. There was a lot of noise coming from the middle of the theatre.

The overhead lights dimmed, and multi-colored lights began streaming across the stage. A young woman in a long, white evening gown came onto the stage. She held a blue envelope.

She smiled as she got to the podium and flipped her red hair back, away from her face. She introduced herself, spoke for a few minutes about the organization that put on the competition and how it started. Then she said: "Now for the show. Our first award is for Best Video."

She opened the envelope, brought out a cardboard card and lowered her head to the microphone again. "The winner is..." She looked down at the card. "Herbology MindWorks!"

The kids jumped up and hugged one other, then turned towards the family members and began hugging them. Moments later they made their way up to the stage.

As producer, director and editor, it was only natural for Herb to be the one to speak. Of course, they all knew that Herb would be the one to speak, no matter if he'd had anything to do with the video.

Zoe was pretty sure that the camera flashes were only concentrated on Herb and his ensemble. He was the star. There was no doubt about that.

Scenes from the video projected onto the wall behind them. Herb, never missing an opportunity to ham it up, rushed up to the images and started mimicking himself, causing a shadow to be cast upon the video. He made it look like an even larger version of himself was haunting his own video self.

He thanked himself (yes, he did...), his bandmates, parents, sister, the other band members' parents and his and Renna's grandmother. However, his gratitude to his grandmother wasn't for the opportunities she gave him or the teachings she imparted. Instead, he thanked her for something she had absolutely nothing to do with.

"I'd also like to thank my grandmother for passing down this glorious hair."

The crowd laughed, eating up Herb's extroversion.

David knew he wasn't ever going to be *that* type of performer. He was a musician, but not an audience-wrangler.

They did not win Best Performance or Best Overall Presentation. Those were both awarded to the same act, predominantly consisting of a fiddler on roller skates with bushy bright blue hair and a massive amount of energy.

In their performance, she had circled the band members (who were rotating on their own part of the stage) as they all played "The Devil Went Down to Georgia." It was carefully coordinated so she'd pass the drummer in between her solos. He'd stick his leg out and she'd jump it. One time he stuck both legs out. The *oohs* from the audience were breathless.

I guess we needed a gimmick, David thought. He didn't really think he'd ever rely on gimmicks. It was just further proof that he'd probably never be a pop culture phenomenon.

Gainesville

Mercedes put her head on the steering wheel. These days it seemed like her sole purpose was to chauffeur her son around. Maybe she wanted to stay home and watch T.V. Maybe she wanted to sleep. Maybe she wanted to clean. No, she never *wanted* to clean. She needed to, though. Her son ambled out of the garage with his guitar. She flicked the garage door opener a few times to let him know she meant business.

"Want me to drive?" he asked, as he set the instrument down in the back seat.

She sighed. Did she want to sleep the hour and a half to Nisha's house? Yes. Did she trust David's not-quite refined driving skills? Did she even need to answer that?

"No," she responded, lifting her head up from the wheel. "I'll drive. Get in the car."

———— • ———— • ————

Nisha lived just outside of Gainesville. She was the only band member already out of school, and she made the drive for band practice one or two times a week, sometimes staying with her cousin who worked for the railroad company.

Her paying job was as a library assistant at the university. She had the time to travel because they only needed her three days a week. She'd gotten the job through her parents, who taught at the school.

Mercedes had asked her one time if she thought about getting a full-time job, only because eventually she'd need things like health insurance. Her answer had been that she hoped her full-time job *would* be the band. After hearing that, Mercedes made sure David knew how much this meant to Nisha. This was her future, and not just a hobby.

She wondered why Nisha didn't play with a local band. Maybe she figured most of the music would be from college bands, and she didn't think college kids would stick around after graduation. Of course she had no way of knowing that high school kids would, either.

Nisha led them out back. Mercedes was impressed with the effort her family had put into the picnic. They'd set up a barbeque in the backyard and had a huge table full of food.

A golden retriever ran by, almost tearing off the tablecloth as she sped by. The youngest Albone, a girl of about eight, ran after her, waving a leash.

Everyone else laughed, but Mercedes backed up toward the fence. She hadn't noticed the man behind her until she was nearly on top of him.

"Excuse me!" Mercedes exclaimed, nearly tipping her cup of lemonade.

The man laughed. "Excuse us. We should put up a sign that says 'Beware of over-exuberant dogs.'"

"Don't get me wrong—I love animals; she just startled me."

"That's Canine Lucy. She runs like she's made of rocket fuel."

"Canine Lucy?" Mercedes asked, surprised. "Are there people who don't know she's a dog, who need a quantifier?"

He hedged a bit, obviously not having an answer ready. Mercedes looked up toward the sliding glass door. A calico cat stared at her from behind the glass.

"Let me guess. Feline Lucy?"

He smiled. "Yeah. She's a diva—loves attention and food. Kitty-Kat Lucy is running around here somewhere. She's the opposite of Feline Lucy—she'd rather be out chasing lizards."

Mercedes' smile withered, and her eyes went cold. "All of your animals are named Lucy?"

He winced. "I should have explained that better. Also, I should have introduced myself. I'm Nisha's uncle, Jonathan. I don't actually live here, but I spend a lot of time here. I'm the on-call babysitter for the kids."

Mercedes slumped. "I'm so sorry. I shouldn't have reacted like that. It is kind of weird...all of the animals having the same name, but I'm sure there's a story there...right?"

He smiled. "Yeah, there's a story there, but it's not very exciting. My brother's youngest daughter, Lucy, insisted that the golden retriever be named Lucy, too. They got Canine Lucy when Girl Lucy was three. Everyone thought it was cute. Then, they got a male cat, and Girl Lucy pitched a fit when her parents wouldn't let her name him Lucy. So, she named him Jack. That's my fault; the family calls me Jack."

"Ahhh..." Mercedes exclaimed. "My family always called me Merche, but we never named the animals that."

"Yeah, so that's the story. Every animal has to have a quantifier."

She clinked the ice in her red cup. "Are you a teacher like your brother and sister-in-law?"

He laughed, nearly choking on his clear soda. "Oh, no. Not at all. My brother hates what I do."

She stared at him, waiting for him to continue.

He shook his head. "Let's get to know each other before you get a chance to judge me, too."

———— • ———— • ————

After everyone had eaten, Nisha came over to the corner lawn chairs Mercedes and Jack were occupying.

"There's a large lake out back. Would you like to watch the sunset from a boat?" Nisha asked Mercedes.

Mercedes shrugged. "Sure. I haven't been out in a boat since—" *Since before my husband left*, she was going to say. "Since last decade sometime. I'd love to."

———— • ———— • ————

David hadn't been in many lakes. There were plenty of rivers and inlets in Jacksonville, but most of the lakes were man made, and belonged to condo complexes and housing subdivisions.

This lake did not look man made, though. The lake shore was craggy; not sculpted like the curated lakes in the neighborhoods he'd visited. He couldn't make out the shore on the other side—all he could see was water and sky. He had to trust that there was an end to the lake. That was an unsettling feeling.

The sharp blue sky was so pure that the light pierced through the atmosphere and seemed to sparkle in the air, and on the water. He noticed a flash of copper glinting far off. The color reminded him of the striated hues of the rock wall in Georgia. On this lake, however, the illusion was due to the sun's rays dancing on the face of the water.

Then he noticed Yvonne. He recognized her from a hundred yards away. He felt a jolt go through him, like a spark of electricity. He was suddenly more aware of everything: the smell of the water, the sounds and silences of the lake, the rolling waves and the unbelievable amount of blue surrounding him.

He sat up from his bored slouch on the seat beside his mother. He tapped Nisha's uncle Jack on the shoulder.

"See that boat up there? I know her. Can we go up there so I can say hello?"

Nisha turned around from the passenger's seat, scrunching her nose. "You're really gonna hit on a girl in the middle of a lake? You see she's with a bunch of guys already."

Jack frowned. "Nisha, if you don't stop acting like a spoiled brat, I'm going to make sure the next round of pets are named after you."

She pouted and folded her arms across her chest, but she didn't protest.

Jack revved the motor up and steered toward the boat. They were about 20 feet away when one of the men (...*boys*, David thought. *Frat boys...*) stood up and made his way to the back of the boat. He started to pull up a rope from the water, but just as he was giving it a hard tug, a small wave crashed against them. The back of the boat swung up like a playground swing. Only it didn't gracefully slide back down to its original position. David stared, petrified, as the boat hung, suspended, and then flipped over, throwing the passengers into the water. He watched Yvonne as she slipped under.

Zoe didn't watch. Zoe threw herself out of David's body. She pushed away from him like she was pushing her own soul toward the light. She pushed herself farther than she ever had. Whatever kept her attached to David must have broken, because she felt like the anchor had been pulled on her own soul. She was light. She could move. She looked back and saw David's horrified face. She looked toward the boat and saw Yvonne struggling to stay afloat.

Zoe continued to push forwards, but she wasn't moving through water. She was above the water. She looked down and saw the ripples. She looked ahead and saw Yvonne bobbing up and down. Every instinct told her to get to her.

Within a minute, she had floated toward the gasping girl. She coaxed the traumatized spirit up, out of the dying body. The body went limp as Zoe pulled the consciousness out.

Then Zoe felt something...someone...grab the body and pull it up. Yvonne's spirit felt it, too, because her soul slipped back into the body. Zoe turned slightly to see part of a long arm pulling the girl towards the Albones' boat.

Zoe turned all the way around. Jack, Nisha's uncle, had saved Yvonne. Zoe was relieved, but, like the upturned boat near her, she felt a little adrift, not sure of her place anymore. She looked back toward David, not feeling the pull anymore. She had about as much a physical connection with him as she did with his mom, as she did with the floating piece of driftwood beside her.

She was free. She was...homeless. Body-less. She drifted back toward David and wedged herself back in, though she felt more like an intruder than ever.

———— • ———— • ————

Mercedes brought David back down to Gainesville a few days later to visit Yvonne in the hospital. Twice now he'd witnessed near-death, and twice it had involved this one specific person. He felt responsible, though he knew he wasn't. The first time had been due to Dempsey's foolishness, and this time to the inexperienced college jerk who'd tried to pull up a stern anchor. He hoped the fates weren't trying to tell Yvonne something. She deserved a long, happy life after everything she'd been through.

She was looking healthier. Her face had gone from ghost-white back to Scottish-pale. Her hair had plumped back up to full-bodied instead of wet-matted. Most importantly, she was smiling. Not a weary smile, but an "I'm happy to see you" smile. David happily reciprocated.

He sat next to her and put his hand on hers. Zoe groaned, awoken by the smell of pheromones in an otherwise sterile environment. *Really?* she thought. *Are you going for a girlfriend in every city?*

David cleared his throat. "How are you feeling?"

Yvonne shrugged. "Better. I shouldn't have been on that boat. I didn't even know those guys. My counselor said I needed to make an effort to connect with other students. Join clubs, be sociable, blah blah blah. I shoulda known it'd get me almost killed."

"Your counselor?" David asked, feeling his heart fall down a flight of stairs. He hadn't realized how much she'd been affected.

This time her smile *was* weary. "Yeah, that episode at camp really did a number on me. I stopped talking to people; I stayed in my bedroom. I didn't even go online anymore. My mother made me apply for college and move down here. At first I thought she just wanted to get rid of me, but I think she was just scared. She didn't want me to be afraid of the world."

David didn't know how to ask this without sounding like an ignorant lug. He tried, anyway. "What was so bad? I mean, I know you almost died, but..." He couldn't think of a logical way to end the sentence.

She shrugged again. She must have been doing a lot of shrugging over the past year. "Before I went to camp, I thought I knew how the world worked. Anything I didn't know could be explained. But that day...what happened...couldn't be explained. I can't tell you what I saw, what I felt. Time stopped for me. *I* stopped, and I never really came back..." She faltered, not sure if she meant that last sentence.

"I don't feel like the same person," she clarified. "There's a hole where certainty used to be. I don't know if I'll ever be able to understand what happened that day, but I'm going to attempt to find out. Instead of just majoring in science, I'm double-majoring—journalism, being my second degree. I'm going to be a science writer. I'm going to get to the bottom of this."

Oh fudge, Zoe thought.

"I bounced back better than Dempsey, though," Yvonne continued. "He's hiding out in his parent's house, rigging stuff up. You know—engineering. He took his GED, like I did. I'm trying to get him to come down here and go to school."

David's face clouded over. "Oh, are you two..."

"We would be," she answered quickly. "If he'd ever leave his house."

Goodbye Zoe

Zoe had never been out on her own before, but she went out now, every night. Breaking away from David was effortless, like breaking a perforation.

She let her instincts guide her. Whether she'd end up at the docks, or at the stadium, she didn't know. Turned out she wasn't ready to leave her area of town. She stopped in front of an older house a few miles away.

The house was at least a hundred years old. Peeling paint revealed a wood frame, and the porch wrapped around to what she could see of the backyard.

The street was quiet, as was the house. It was three o'clock in the morning. No neighbors were bustling in their yards, no cars were racing down the street, angering the parents of young children. Not even the dogs were barking, which surprised Zoe. She'd figured they'd sense her presence and alert their owners. But no, they must have been used to the appearance of grim reapers.

That phrase surprised her. She'd never put a name to what she was. Was she a grim reaper? She'd never been issued a scythe. She didn't own a black cloak, but that was probably because she didn't have a body to put it on.

She looked around. Why was she at this house? Why did she feel this urge to go in? She didn't feel right trespassing in the middle of the night. She'd have to wait until later.

———— • —— • ————

She wasn't ready to tell David that she could float away whenever she wanted. She wasn't sure how he'd take it. He depended on her to remember their locker combination, and what night their favorite shows came on. Plus, knowing that she could rotate in and out of his head might freak him out.

She left on a Saturday morning. That way he'd have most of the day to adjust to her absence. She'd be back long before band practice. She'd break the news gently to him.

She made sure she was mobile long before he woke up. She scarcely had to navigate to the old house. Her mind—or whatever her consciousness was called—followed the steps like she was being towed.

This time the block was alive. Men and women tended gardens and mowed yards. Young kids played basketball in the street. A mail truck lurched from box to box, stopping at each one to deliver that week's heap of coupons and sales papers.

She looked toward the house. She saw movement through the windows. Her heart lurched like the mail truck. She saw a woman through the curtains, looking out at her, and then turning back toward the living room.

Zoe went up to the window. Placing her hand up to the glass, she realized she could push through it like an oar pushing through water. First her hand, then her arm, and soon she was standing in the living room. The woman was sitting on a loveseat, staring at her. Her eyes were hard and cautious.

Zoe had never been able to look in a mirror, but looking at this woman, she felt like she was looking at an older version of herself. Somewhere maybe there was a body waiting for her with a tall, strong frame like this woman's.

A younger woman interrupted the standoff, oblivious to Zoe's infiltration. "We're going to take care of Annalisa."

The woman nodded, not taking her eyes off of Zoe. "Do everything...hair, nails, all of it."

The young woman furrowed her eyebrows. "What? Is she graduating from high school? Winning a prize? That'll take all day."

The woman flipped her eyes from Zoe to the young woman. "Charise, I wouldn't ask you if there wasn't a reason."

The young woman turned and walked toward a hallway. Zoe followed her to a bedroom in the middle of the house. Another young woman about the same age was washing someone in a hospital bed. She held a washcloth to the forehead, but the person wasn't moving at all.

She listened as the two women talked about the older woman's orders. They didn't sound happy about all the work it would entail. Zoe wasn't sure if they saw the person in the bed as a person anymore, or as a chore.

The door to the house was old, and wooden, but it must have been strong. They were startled by a knock that pierced all the way to the bedroom. The two women gasped and began covering the unconscious body in the bed. Zoe felt their panic, and suddenly felt very disoriented. She couldn't tell if she was spinning or the room was spinning, because she didn't have a body to judge it by.

Only, she did have a body. She felt the hot air in the room rush by her, and then felt the coolness of freshly washed cotton sheets covering her. She felt the firmness of a mattress beneath her. She'd been aware of these sensations before, but she'd never really *felt* them. Not for herself, anyway.

—————— • —————— • ——————

Annalisa's mother shushed the two younger women, and nodded toward the back of the house. She waited as long as she dared before opening the door to Laura, the officious Councilwoman.

Laura pushed her way in, looking around the small living room and peering down the hallway. She opened her mouth before Annalisa's mother had a chance to protest.

"You know you can't have more than two children alive. Is this why your daughters don't work as much as the other Soulpushers?

They don't have enough power because a third child is sharing their abilities?"

The mom looked straight at her. "I only have two children."

"Oh, really? So if I look back through your house, I won't find anyone else?"

Mrs. Zearott regretted not renting an apartment for Annalisa and the girls to stay in. Would that have remained a secret, though? Would she have still faced this moment? She tried to harden her face so that no expression showed. That probably made her look more odd and nervous.

Zoe wasn't sure if she could move, even if she wanted to. She'd never directed movement in her own body before. So she stayed frozen—at least until the two women started lifting her. Apparently she didn't like being grappled, so she started fidgeting and kicked one of the women.

The woman released her, and she fell hard on the bed. The other one ran out as swiftly (but quietly) as she could and returned with a cart. They had a time getting Zoe's struggling body strapped to it. Zoe's voice wasn't working quite yet, so the groan that escaped sounded more like a phlegmy cough. They pushed her out into the backyard, and settled her next to a grill. There was just enough room under the grill cover to mask Zoe's huddled body.

"You gotta be kidding me," she phlegm-coughed.

During the two months that Zoe needed for physical recovery, she didn't leave her mother's house. Her two sisters had kept her muscles from atrophying, but that didn't mean she was ready to go dancing. She would take small trips to the bathroom (another of nature's tasks she had to learn), but she wasn't ready to stand in the shower. She had to learn how to speak, and how to eat. Her body didn't take too well to whole food (which wrapped back around to that task she was still learning).

No amount of gifts could assuage Mrs. Zearott's guilt in having bunted her daughter's soul into another body, but she tried. She bought Zoe a tablet computer. Zoe spent most of her time reading every book, and playing every game her mother had loaded onto it.

Putting on clothes was a new activity. She didn't show any interest in the blouses, slacks and dresses her sisters brought back. Instead, they gave Zoe their hand-me-downs. The older sisters had different body types than Zoe, but also being on bed rest for 16 years meant Zoe's body was smaller and less developed than it would have been. The clothes hung from her shoulders, but she made do. She didn't like bras, but understood that society did, so she wore them, uncomfortably.

She asked her newly-found family to call her Zoe, and not Annalisa. She preferred sticking with the name she'd given herself, rather than the one given to her by the person who'd kicked her to the spiritual curb. She didn't say this, though, because she accepted that her mother had acted in what she thought was Zoe's best interest.

Zoe thought about David every day. Was he adjusting to life without her? Was he looking at music colleges? Would he be able to pass the SAT? Did he miss her?

Goodnight David

Parshall adjusted David's IV line. She'd had to pull what little influence she had to keep him there. Long term patients tended to get transferred. She felt responsible, though, and no amount of influence could undo what she'd done by tipping off Laura. The head Councilwoman had visited a house suspected of harboring a third child. This had been the same day David hadn't woken up. Something must have happened that day to pull the hijacker back into her own body.

"So...it must be weird having no one in there with you," she said, pulling his bed sheet up a little. She felt the lameness of her comment as soon as she said it, but she didn't know what else to say. She didn't know the spirit that had departed...she didn't even know the name. Come to think of it, she didn't even know David. She knew he liked music, but she didn't know what kind. So, she chose for him.

She picked up the music player someone had docked in a small speaker system. It was Wi-Fi enabled, so she went to her online music account and picked a song that was heartfelt, but not in a romantic way. She found Carole King's "You've got a friend."

Beneath Carole's breathy voice she heard shuffling. She didn't remember that from the song. She turned around and saw two of David's friends working their way hesitantly through the door. They looked a little unsure about intruding.

Parshall rose and walked over to them, extending her hand. The young man shook it, looking around at anything but Parshall.

The young woman with the brilliant red hair looked directly at Parshall, but gasped the moment she caught sight of her eyes. Something in her eyes was familiar.

Parshall jumped back. She knew exactly what had happened. *This girl has seen a Soulpusher before.* She nervously clutched the player, trying to turn the music up. Instead, she just managed to skip to the next song. She pushed hard on the off button, forcing it to power down.

She ran past them, but the young woman caught her arm.

"Please," the girl begged. "Tell me what you are."

Zoe Zearott Investigates

Zoe had no idea where to start. She wasn't supposed to officially exist, so she didn't want to draw much attention to herself. Still, she wanted to learn more about the Council and the history of soul-pushing. Laura, the leader of the organization, had it in for her family. She didn't know if it was an old family rivalry, or if her grudge was because of some slight she had perceived from her mother. She didn't know how it started, but she wanted it ended. Her sisters and her mother deserved that.

She used the computer at the local library, so as to not connect her family. She started with researching supernatural phenomena. She found all she hoped to know on UFOs, ghosts, Sasquatch, clairvoyance, past lives, and doppelgangers.

Nostradamus predicted two World Wars, but the jury was still out on whether the wars had already occurred. Old Nessie may have been dead—the last of her kind, at the bottom of Lake Ness.

She found a paranormal society that was looking for a new member. *Hmmm...*she thought. *I'll need some sort of vocation eventually, though I don't think I'd get paid.*

But nothing of Soulpushing. It must have been the most well-kept secret on Earth.

She found one article about a supposed ghost figure captured in a hospital ward. The photographer swore he had been alone in the hallway. When someone asked why he was taking a picture of an empty corridor, he said it was to show his elderly father. The dad had been telling anyone who'd listen that there were dozens of people traipsing up and down the hall at night, disturbing him. Minutes after the picture was taken, the father had died.

Zoe looked hard at the figure. It looked to be wearing scrubs, so the person most likely worked there. She knew that a lot of pushers worked at hospitals. That way they avoided travel time, and no one questioned their continual presence. She bet they learned how to be quiet and unobtrusive, too. So stealthy that a person who happened to notice might think they were a ghost.

She started thinking about where else Soulpushers might be concentrated. In the military, she thought. The sadness of that struck her. They would most likely be deployed to war zones. The unseen patrol.

She needed to stay clear of official Soulpushing channels…get answers from someone outside of Arlington's network. Someone with ties to the old world, and old traditions.

David's mother didn't have any family there. Zoe wished Mercedes' mother were still alive; she'd been steeped in Puerto Rico's religious and cultural tapestry.

However, thanks to Mercedes, Zoe understood Spanish. Zoe knew what to do.

———————— • ———— • ————

Well, she had an idea of where to start. Mrs. Byres had mostly bought groceries at the big grocery store. However, when her mother visited, her shopping switched to the Puerto Rican grocery down the street. The old woman who worked the register would raise her eyebrows when they walked in, murmur a barely audible "uh huh," and whisper something about mama must be in town.

Zoe didn't know if the woman knew anything about Soulpushers. She had to try, though. She'd hit a brick wall at the library. The internet was surprisingly hush hush about the phenomenon, and it wasn't in any books she found.

She went to the candy aisle because growing up that's all David had been interested in. She knew that layout. She swiped a glance toward the counter up front. Yep, the same lady was there. She was watching a news broadcast on a laptop. It looked like something from WKAQ.

The show started buffering and the woman started hitting the monitor, as if all she needed to do was adjust the antenna.

Zoe grabbed her candy and grabbed her opportunity.

"Señora, con permiso, ¿le puedo hacer una pregunta?"

The woman stared at her. "Just one question? I think you need to ask many. Your Spanish is terrible. Have you ever spoken the language before?"

Zoe burned with embarrassment. She realized she'd never spoken the language. She'd only heard it. She tried again. Her Spanish was as wooden as an old workman's bench.

"Me llamo Zoe."

The woman pushed her hands out toward Zoe, as if pushing the words back. "Parada. You are not allowed to use Spanish in this store. Those are the right words, but you're mangling them. What do you want? I haven't seen you before."

Zoe hung her head. She thought her Puerto Rican Spanish was spot-on, but apparently this woman expected perfection. "I would like to know about our culture...your culture..."

The woman looked sideways at her. "What are you?"

Zoe dropped her head down on the conveyor belt. She rose up in shock as the motor started. The cashier pushed the stop button.

"You've even angered the machine. You don't feel right to me. There's something wrong with you."

Zoe looked absolutely defeated...too drained to stand up and walk out. She kept leaning against the temperamental station.

"Did you ever hear about people who could draw spirits out of people?"

The woman backed up. "Like a shaman?"

"No. Not like a shaman. I'm sorry. I'm not explaining this very well. People who can pull souls out of people and send them to heaven."

The woman stared at Zoe, thinking she was playing a prank...probably recording this for the internet. Some kind of "Latina lady talks crazy magic" story.

Zoe didn't give up, though. She stayed collapsed on the conveyor belt, looking up pleadingly at the cashier. She really needed something, and it wasn't gum or candy.

The woman softened her expression. "I did hear stories, when I was a child. My grandfather was dying. My grandmother called for someone. I thought it was a priest, but the person who came wasn't a priest. I remember my father was furious. He said he didn't want witchcraft in the house. Never seen my grandmother so defiant. She refused to let papa into the bedroom. She'd only let the lady in.

"In the last few moments papa did sneak the priest in. When the door opened, we saw the woman in front of the bed, raising her arms. We saw light going up to the ceiling. The woman was smiling, with her eyes closed. She had her arms raised like she was conducting an orchestra.

"Later, after the funeral, I asked Abuela about the woman. She said the woman guided Abuelo's soul to Heaven. She pushed the soul out, so it wasn't staying past its time."

Zoe was crying. "I'm like that woman. But I don't know how to do it. Not right, anyway. I'm a feral Soulpusher. I don't know how to find the people I'm supposed to help."

The cashier gasped, staring at her. "Well, no wonder you're so odd. My name is Luisa, and I'll help you. I'm an old lady. I know lots of dying people. You can start with my sister, Adora."

———— • —— • ————

Zoe hadn't been to the hospital since Grandmother Byres had died. She wasn't prepared for just how bright the halls were...just how strong the smell of cleaning detergent was. She'd experienced all of those sensations second hand before.

Luisa knocked on one of the hospital room doors. There wasn't an answer, but she entered anyway. Zoe trailed in behind her, keeping her distance—worried she'd step on the oxygen or medicine line. The last thing she wanted to do was sever this poor woman's life sustenance.

Adora was lying on the bed. She was older than Luisa. Her thinned-out silver hair gathered behind her head. The lines in her skin all pointed toward her mouth. Zoe had imagined Luisa as the rambunctious one, so she figured Adora's frown lines were from a lifetime of chiding her younger sister, constantly telling Luisa not to play with lizards.

Zoe gave up trying to understand their conversation. Their Spanish flew out of their mouths at double speed. She heard her name a few times, and both women gestured to her with each sentence. Zoe became uncomfortable. How much did Luisa have to say about her?

The sister finally paused and looked at her. "Am I ready to go now? Is my soul ready?"

Zoe's brain seized up. Was she supposed to be on call? This must have been that performance anxiety she'd heard the band talk about. She couldn't move and couldn't speak. She wouldn't know what to say anyway, even if she could speak.

By the Cover of Night

Parshall paused, hoping the kids would go away. If there was a pusher doghouse, she was in it. Letting an outsider recognize her abilities...that was a Council write-up. All she could hope for was that they didn't find out. To ensure that, she'd probably have to talk to them.

She turned around quickly toward Yvonne "I don't know what you think you felt, or saw, but I'm just a regular nurse. I work seven to seven, three nights a week. For fun I like to go to movies and play trivia at the local pizza place. I only have a few friends, though, and no one ever wants to go with me. It's very sad. But it's normal. *I'm* normal."

Yvonne looked at her. "We'll go to trivia with you..."

Parshall stared back at her, not knowing what to say.

Yvonne continued. "...if you help us find out what happened to us and our friend."

Parshall looked at their faces. She could tell they were in pain. They didn't look like exposé writers, or undercover Council spies. She thought about the pizza at her favorite trivia spot. She really missed that pizza. Why did she feel weird going alone? Oh yeah. It was awkward if she didn't win, and even more awkward if she did win.

She thought about the Council. It had always seemed like they were there to constrict the pushers...to tell them how to do their jobs. She already got that from the doctors. She didn't need it with her unpaid second job.

"Trivia first, and then information."

Trivia

The pizza place was a few miles from the hospital. It had sprouted up with dozens of other trendy chain restaurants in the shinier part of town—the part so new that it looked like it was made up of Lego blocks.

This place bucked the trend, though. She loved the murals all across the walls, and the eclectic beer selection. The restaurant was always crowded with happy, chattering people. Maybe that's what she liked so much. Even though she was usually sitting at the bar with nothing but her e-books, she always felt like she was part of the bustle.

Parshall knew she came off as condemning the suburbanites. She wasn't, though. She was envious. She'd love to live in an apartment newer than her car. She'd love to smell new paint, rather than old must. But the Council wanted all their subjects to stay close to their beat.

Her apartment wasn't awful. It was room enough for her, and near the stores she went to most. She just wanted the freedom to live in the upscale side of town. The billboards all promised a life that went beyond shopping for BOGOs at the grocery store.

She'd forgotten how long it could take to get a table. The line was out the door, which meant they'd get a table around the half-time point. She couldn't even plan trivia night right. She thought about texting the two kids and suggesting the beer pub down the street, but then she remembered they were kids. Probably 17. *Stupid laws*, she thought.

Just then she noticed the lankiest object she'd ever seen waving from one of the restaurant's windows. Oh, that was the kid...Dempsey. They must have been there for half an hour, to have a table already.

———— • —— • ————

"An hour. We went ahead and ate, since we wanted to have table space for the scratch paper. We brought ten sheets. Do you think that'll be enough?"

Parshall stared at the girl. They were taking this trivia thing way more seriously than she ever did. She usually just scribbled her notes on napkins.

She was surprised they showed up at all. Honoring promises seemed like a dying virtue to her. She was trying to be happy, but there was just so much weird to break through.

She decided to start with the trivia game. She was good at science, but she wasn't an expert by any stretch. Yvonne was ready with every answer, though. They didn't even have to deliberate. Turned out Dempsey was a house of knowledge when it came to engineering and architecture.

Not having to deliberate their answers left lots of open minutes for the two younger people to grill Parshall about her ability. Parshall was grateful that she hadn't already eaten. She filled as many open minutes as she could with the sound of her munching on pizza.

Yvonne was the first with a question for Pusher Trivia night.

"I should have died that day on the lake. All I could see was water, then the sky, and then this haze. More than seeing, though, I could feel it pulling me. I was ready to let go of my struggle and go toward it. Whatever it was, it came from David. And now he's lying unresponsive in a hospital room. Did I do that to him? Can I fix it?"

Dempsey was quiet. He didn't strike Parshall as the wallflower type, but he was looking down at his hands and fidgeting the whole time Yvonne was talking. Whatever happened to him, it must have affected him more.

The trivia master's voice in the speakers called Parshall's attention back into the noisy room.

"Next category is science. Name the two ingredients commonly used to make potassium chlorate."

Yvonne and Dempsey looked like a ghost had just reached over and stolen the Parmesan jar. Yvonne's hands were shaking as she picked up the pencil and wrote "bleach" and "salt-free sodium" on the slip of paper. She didn't seem capable of moving, so Parshall took the answer up to the booth.

Yvonne looked after her, her eyes red and swollen. "What are you?"

Another One Like Zoe

Zoe fielded more questions from more people who were convinced the time was nigh. She didn't get any sense that their mortal coils were bending, much less breaking.

An alarm went off in the hallway. Zoe jumped up and ran out. Doctors and nurses were running toward a room. She heard the muffled sounds of a machine, and a voice yelling "clear."

She felt breath on her back—tobacco breath. Her sense of smell was sharper now that she had her own sense of smell.

She looked back to see Luisa trying to edge past her.

"That's the kid's room. He's only been here two days. Poor kid."

"What's wrong with him?" Zoe asked.

"Nothing. Well, nothing physical, until now. Adora hears the doctors talking. They don't know what's wrong with him. His brain is fine. He just won't wake up."

She looked at Zoe. "Hey...maybe you'd better go see if he needs a little help."

Zoe blanched. She wasn't ready for this. "Why would they let me in? I don't work here. Besides, I'm sure there's a real Soulpusher around here."

Luisa frowned. "You are a real Soulpusher. Figure out a way to get close."

She rolled her eyes. "I'm going to get kicked out."

The doctors were still working on the patient. He really wasn't a kid—he was older than Zoe. Probably in his 20's. He was pale, and the only moving he did was the involuntary jerks from the defibrillator slamming down on his chest.

She started thinking about what it was like on the lake...what she had done to draw out Yvonne's spirit.

She closed her eyes and raised her arms. She felt out for his soul. She felt the edges of the nurses' souls...all healthy and intact. She pushed toward the bed with her mind. She felt the warmth of the young man's blood, and the heat of the machine. Underneath, though, she felt nothing. Life began and ended with blood, arteries and the heart that was failing.

Her eyes snapped open. There wasn't a soul there to push.

———— • —— • ————

"What do you know about him?" Zoe asked.

She'd run back to Adora's room as soon as she'd realized what she was dealing with.

Adora shrugged from her place in the hospital bed. "Not much, personally. I know who he is, though. He's the son of that big time contractor. You know—the one who built all those buildings. He's dead now. You may have seen him on the other side."

She looked up at Zoe. "You can go up to Heaven, yes? Can you see our mama? Ask her where she put her fine jewelry? I never could find it. I don't want to sell it. I just want to wear it."

Zoe looked exasperated and bewildered. Luisa admonished her sister. "Zoe can't go up to Heaven. It doesn't work that way. Besides, where are you going to wear jewelry? The cafeteria?"

Adora lowered her head, as if in reverence to a higher power. "The chapel, dear sister. If I'm going to meet our Father soon, I want to look my best."

Luisa rolled her eyes. "Our Father has seen you at your best, and your worst. Trust me—he probably doesn't see a difference."

Adora raised her head sharply to Luisa. "Are you saying there is no difference between my best and my worst?"

"Ah, dear sister. Only the Lord truly knows."

Zoe cleared her throat. The sisters were still staring at each other, as if daring the other to speak. Luisa turned to Zoe.

"Yes?" Luisa asked, starting to feel like she was being admonished by a 16-year-old girl.

"The contractor?" Zoe reminded her.

"Oh yes!" Luisa exclaimed, looking over at Adora. "You remember more about that because you were at home watching television, while I worked at the store."

Adora's face reddened as she rose up in bed. "I had surgery! I had to stay home!" She looked nervously over at Zoe, and then lowered back into the bed. "Yes, I do remember. It was all over the 12 o'clock news. The boy's father had been contracted to build a riverwalk. He abruptly pulled out of the contract, though, saying he had been coerced into using faulty materials. Just as the city got involved, the man's wife gave birth to the boy down the hall. He was born in the same condition he's in now. He wasn't brain dead; he had some activity—just not much."

Adora continued. "This took its toll on the family. The wife took all of her time caring for the boy, in addition to hiring a live-in nurse. The father lost his will to run the company. He closed the doors, and soon after he died. The mother and nurse took care of the boy until the mother died recently." She gestured to Zoe to lean in closely. "Rumor is the mother left the estate to the nurse. There wasn't much money left, but enough for her to live on and pay taxes, if she invested well."

"Then why is he here?" Zoe asked.

"I don't really know—"

"...but that's never stopped you from guessing," Luisa interrupted.

One sharp look from her older sister hushed her.

"I don't really know," Adora continued, "but my guess is they're getting legal matters tied up. The house is in bad repair, I know, and the Disability and Health Program is requiring upgrades to the house. That all takes time and money. So, the money has to get sorted before the time can be spent. Meanwhile, this poor kid is here."

Zoe thought for a moment. What could have happened to leave a baby without a soul? Well, her own situation came to mind. Did someone else know how to push a soul into another living body? Or is her mother the only one? Another thought seized her. Had her mother done this?

"Does the nurse come to visit?" Zoe asked Adora.

Adora laughed. "Oh, sweetie. The hospital was kind enough to give the nurse a temporary job here so that she could pay for an apartment. She's here almost every day.

Well, that made Zoe's job a little easier. She knew exactly where to start.

Dempsey, Yvonne and Parshall: Private Detectives (Not for Hire)

"So you have the whole week off?" Dempsey asked Parshall. They were sitting in Parshall's living room while Yvonne was in the kitchen, making arrangements with her teachers to have the assignments that weren't already online emailed to her.

"Yeah, it was the weirdest thing. The other day the HR rep said that the hospital had done an audit and found four days of leave that had supposedly been lost years ago. Then she said that they had a new nurse starting, and she needed the hours, so could I take my leave now? I said sure. I knew we were doing this, so I didn't argue."

Dempsey shrugged. "Luckily I don't do anything, so I didn't have anybody to ask."

He looked so defeated that Parshall felt really sorry for him. "I know that Yvonne wants you to go to the university with her," she suggested.

"Yeah. She does. I'm just not sure I can handle it."

"Can you do online classes?"

He perked up a little. "Yeah. Not everywhere offers an Engineering degree online, but she's going to help me find somewhere. Wherever it is, we have to make sure it's accredited. It's more expensive to go to school online. I'm hoping that if I start off that way, maybe eventually I'll be ready for in person."

Parshall smiled. He didn't seem to realize he'd said "we," meaning he and Yvonne.

———— • ———— • ————

The hardest part of the plan was deciding what day and time to do it. No one had a really good understanding of what the hours were for the Council headquarters. There wasn't a sign on the door. Dempsey thought they should wait until the dead of night, because that's when all nefarious activity was done. Yvonne said that wasn't true; after all, stockbrokers and politicians worked during the day. Parshall suggested that they do some recon work on Laura Altmeyer. She was the only Council employee that Parshall even knew about. She also reluctantly agreed to stay home because Laura would too easily sniff out another Soulpusher.

Yvonne drove herself and Dempsey to the Council building at 5 AM, but they parked at a nearby breakfast shop. They went into the restaurant and Dempsey kept his eyes on the parking lot as Yvonne ordered. Three cups of coffee (and numerous strips of bacon, pieces of toast and grains of grits) later, they saw Laura's sedan pull up. They watched as she unlocked the door and went in.

After throwing away their trash and going outside, they moved their car around to the back of the sandwich shop. The hope was that if Laura looked out the window, she wouldn't see the same car parked for hours. From their vantage point, they still saw her car.

They waited, the thought sinking in that they could be waiting like that all day.

"I have to pee," Yvonne stated, matter-of-factly.

"I brought a jug," Dempsey stated, matter-of-factly.

Yvonne didn't know what he meant at first, so she waited for him to say more.

"EWWWW," she exclaimed, understanding what he meant. "You're paying to have the car cleaned if you miss!"

An hour later, out of desperation, Yvonne went into the laundromat next door to use their restroom. She would have gone back to the restaurant, but she didn't want to let on that they were camping out all day. She bought two sodas from the vending machine for her and Dempsey, guaranteeing that she'd be back to use their restroom. *The circle of life*, she thought.

When she got back to the car, Dempsey was really excited.

"What?" she asked, handing him the can. "What's got you in such a tizzy?"

"What's a tizzy?" he asked, still jumping up and down in his seat.

"Never mind. It's something my grandmother used to say. Sometimes I forget what generation I'm from. What are you so excited about?"

"The lady. Laura. She went out to the bus stop and got on a bus!"

Yvonne almost dropped her soda. She recovered it just in time. "Did you see what bus?"

The grin faded a bit. "What do you mean 'what bus'? Isn't there just one?"

She groaned, and pointed at the bus stop. The bus had three numbers, each representing a bus Laura Altmeyer could have taken.

———— • —— • ————

Luckily for them, Parshall answered their phone call.

"What do you mean she's gone?"

Yvonne glanced over at Dempsey, sipping his soda. "The great observer here failed to take note of what bus she got on."

Yvonne heard a lot of static, and it seemed like Parshall might have dropped the phone.

"Hold on," Parshall called out to the phone.

More static, and then "Ok. Got it. One of the nurses takes the bus. She told me about an app that tells you what buses are coming and where they're going. I'm downloading it now. When did you say it left?"

Yvonne looked over at Dempsey again. He pretended he couldn't hear Parshall through the speaker. Yvonne sighed. "I was away for about 5 minutes. So, we'll say between five and ten minutes ago."

Silence again, then some rustling as Parshall brought her phone down. "Ok, I put you on speaker. Can you hear me?"

Dempsey muttered yes. Yvonne nodded, and then felt stupid when she realized Parshall couldn't hear a nod.

"Ok. The 50 is the last bus that came by. It left your area about eight minutes ago, going west. How about this: You both try to catch up with the bus. I'll ride over and babysit the Council building to make sure no one else goes in."

———— • —— • ————

They stopped at a red light. The bus was a block ahead. They had no way of knowing if Laura had already gotten off.

They were in luck. They were able to see Laura get off the bus and see the direction she was headed in. They kept an eye on her until they were sure she went into a standalone restaurant. Yvonne turned into the parking lot and drove to the back corner, hoping Laura hadn't looked out the window and seen their car.

They waited.

Yvonne texted Parshall with an update.

The cell phone rang, startling Dempsey awake, and causing Yvonne to shake donut powder dust onto her lap. Yvonne answered the phone with a sugary flick of her finger.

They could hear the laughter before Yvonne had a chance to say hello.

"Yes," she asked.

"I figured out what she's doing there."

"The anticipation's too much," Yvonne answered back.

"It's happy hour there. Two to seven. No telling how long she'll be there."

"Well, we still need to wait, right?" Yvonne asked.

"Yeah, probably. We need to keep eyes on both locations. I'll tell ya what. Pizza's on me whenever you're done for the night. I'll babysit the Council building after she goes home...if she ever goes home."

Yvonne sighed. Dempsey coughed. She handed him some of her water. He spit it out.

"What," she whispered to him. "I can't drink soda all day like you do."

Parshall cleared her throat, reminding them that she was still there. "Call me as soon as she leaves for the bus stop."

Yvonne hung up. She looked at her watch. They'd been there almost two hours. How long was she going to stay there? Was this her version of work? *Nice gig*, she thought.

Just then she saw Laura approach the exit. She nudged Dempsey back awake. They both watched as Laura fought with the door a little. The door ultimately let Laura through, but her scarf got caught on the handle. Laura didn't notice. Instead, she walked toward the bus stop, scarfless.

The two amateur detectives looked at each other. They both smiled, then looked at the scarf. Dempsey got out of the car and ran toward the door, while Yvonne looked after Laura, hoping she didn't turn around.

Once at the door, Dempsey grabbed the scarf and went into the restaurant. He got the attention of the person at the register.

"Sir, sir! Hi! Yes, the woman who just left dropped her scarf." He held it up toward the employee.

The employee took the scarf, smiling. "Thanks! I'll give this to Laura tomorrow."

Dempsey raised his eyebrows. "Tomorrow...?"

"Yeah. She comes here every day at two. She stays until she feels up to walking to the bus stop."

"Every day?"

"Every weekday. Has been for years."

"Huh," Dempsey said. "Thanks...for taking the scarf, that is."

"No problem," the employee said. "You look too young for happy hour, but you'd probably like our food." He handed Dempsey a coupon.

Dempsey took it. "Thanks," he called out, running toward the door.

A Soul Separated

Renna sat at David's bedside, thinking she must be the most loyal non-girlfriend ever. She'd had months to deliberate it. If he woke up, she'd swear her love to him for always and ever. If he didn't wake up...what would she do? How long would she sit there?

She talked to him like he was there, but he didn't move. Didn't acknowledge her.

"Andrew got invited to perform in a Mardi Gras parade. I told him to do it. The band's still together...still practicing. They pulled in one of Nisha's friends from Gainesville to play guitar..."

Just as she finished her sentence, the table at the end of the bed began rattling. Instinctively she pulled back her words.

"It's ok," she backtracked. "It's just temporary. She knows you'll be coming back."

The table wasn't the only thing rattled by that incident. Renna nervously looked around, and then ran out the room, down the hall, and down the stairs.

Jack Albone

Jack wasn't happy with the hospital coffee. The powdered creamer looked like household cleaner. The paper cups were thin and not doing a good job of protecting his hands from the sharp heat. He wondered how many of their emergencies originated from that cafeteria.

He was distracted by a blur coming at him. It was David's friend Renna. She'd been sitting with David while he and Mercedes were getting dinner.

"What is it?" he asked, as she got closer.

She stopped to catch her breath. "Where's Mercedes?"

"She's getting our food. We've been alternating paying...why?"

She gasped again and leaned over, holding her head in her hands. "I gotta go."

She skulked out, leaving a baffled Jack holding a scalding cup. He remembered that he was in pain and set the cup on the table.

———— • ———— • ————

Zoe entered through the front lobby. She wasn't sure where to start. The cafeteria was on the right—she figured that was as good a place as any.

She'd seen a picture of the nurse in the paper, but it had been grainy. She scanned the tables. Plenty of people in scrubs, but no one with the same hairstyle and build as the woman in the photo.

Someone did stand out, but it wasn't a nurse. It was the man from the Albones' party. Zoe tried to clear up her memory. It had been so many months ago, and she hadn't been herself when she (or rather David) had met him.

She remembered some things about him, though. He'd been cagey about what he did for a living. Also, the space around him had felt different. Fuller. She'd had a similar feeling when she'd met her family for the first time.

She rushed up to him, not thinking through a plan.

"Mr. Albone?" she sputtered, nearly crashing into the table.

Really? he thought. *Accosted at a hospital?* "Do I know you?" he answered out loud.

She froze. She wasn't really sure. Did she know him?

He continued before she had a chance to flounder more. "Did we meet at a convention?"

"Um...sort of. I mean, there were people there...and they were convening."

Albone seemed OK with the explanation. "Did you have any questions for me?"

She took a leap of faith, trusting her instincts. "You study weird stuff, right?"

He laughed. "Well, I don't think it's so weird. Ghosts, telekinesis, strange places—"

Ha! She had guessed right! "Yeah, yeah, yeah. Have you ever heard of people who can push other people's souls to the other side?"

He froze mid-coffee sip. "How do you know about that?"

She wasn't prepared for his alarmed reaction. "Uh...uh...I don't know. How do *you* know about that?" Zoe hadn't been active in the world long enough to know that turning a question around on someone rarely worked.

"I asked you first."

"Uh...I suppose I should re-introduce myself. My name is Zoe, and I push souls to the spirit realm. Or, at least that's what I'm supposed to be doing. The Council kinda clipped my wings early on. I'm not a big fan of theirs."

"You're right not to trust the Council. You know this is the only city that has a formal system? They claim it's because they have so few Soulpushers. The problem is that when Jacksonville consolidated decades ago, the Council brought in all of the rural areas. They should have let the outer towns and suburbs take care of their own, like they had been doing. Now those pushers are furious because most of their people get assigned to the city core. I understand there are a lot of hospitals here, but people are still dying in the country."

"Plus they only let two Soulpusher children per family," Zoe noted quietly.

He responded quietly also. "That's the touchiest subject. I've been trying to find out what they do with any third kids born. Do they siphon the power out of them? Send them away?"

He doesn't know, she thought. She wasn't sure if that made her feel better or worse. It explained why outsiders didn't intervene. They didn't know how twisted the practices were.

"If you help me, I'll tell you everything I know, and we'll find out the rest," she suggested.

He nodded. "I'd like that very much. I've had a bad feeling about this Council for years—ever since I found out about them." He took a sip of coffee. "Would you like something to eat or drink?"

She shook her head. "I need to get upstairs."

"Oh, ok. I was wondering if you were just stalking me, or if you're visiting someone," he said jokingly.

She nodded, not picking up on his attempt at lightheartedness. She didn't want to elaborate, so she switched the topic back to him. "Who are you here to visit?" she asked. This time the bait and switch worked.

"That's a sad and perplexing story. There's a boy in a coma—"

"Oh!" Zoe interrupted, a little too excitedly. "I heard about him! You're going to visit him?"

Jack looked annoyed. "I know you're not the most socially adept person, Zoe, but please don't act so excited when you're talking about someone's misfortune."

She lowered her head. "I'm sorry. I'm not good at being tactful. I'll get out of your way now."

He stopped her as she was standing up. He dug in his pocket and brought out a business card. He handed it to her. "Call me, OK?"

———— • ———— • ————

Zoe leaned back against the wall as she waited for the elevator. The door dinged and opened. When she got up to the boy's room, he was still lying in the same position. His blonde hair was cut short, and she noted how pale and fragile he looked.

She walked in and stood near the young man, wondering what to do next. A noise behind her answered her question. The nurse had come to her.

"What are you doing in here? Get out of here. Haven't you people done enough to him? You have his soul. You want his body, too?"

Zoe choked, rushing to explain that she wasn't the bad guy. "I didn't do anything to him. I'm new to all this. I just want to find out what happened. I want to make sure it doesn't happen to anyone else."

The nurse paused. "Do you know where he is?"

Zoe choked on her words again. "No...I mean, what? Of course I know where he is. He's right here!"

The nurse huffed. "You know what I mean. Do you know where his soul is? I've been trying to find it for almost twenty years."

Zoe was shocked. She knew his soul wasn't in there? She knew about the Council?

"Are you a pusher?" Zoe asked, her voice breaking a little with trepidation.

"No. If I were, I'd probably know where his soul was, wouldn't I?" she answered, exasperation flooding her voice.

"Maybe not. I'm a Soulpusher, but I have no idea where his soul is."

The nurse relented a little. Fighting this girl wasn't going to help.

"Whoever set this up knew what they were doing. They brought a host from the outside. I've investigated every other child that was in the hospital when he was born. I've looked into the families, in case his soul was in one of the parents or siblings. Nothing. Whoever got his soul didn't sign in at the front desk."

Zoe moved a little closer to the nurse. She put her hand on the nurse's hand. "I promise I'll do my best to find his soul. I want to put him back where he belongs."

"Do you think he'd be OK? Do you think he'd be whole again?"

Zoe nodded. "I think he would."

"Good. Because he's not the only one like him here."

Dempsey, Yvonne and Parshall Break into the Council

The three wanna-be intruders discovered that there was no sure time Laura would be gone, except for her daily excursion to happy hour. They waited until after the sun had gone down that first evening, but Laura's car never moved. Parshall let Yvonne and Dempsey go home, but she stayed until early in the morning. The next night Laura left at 6 P.M., but Parshall stuck around to make sure Laura was gone for the night. No dice. Laura came back around midnight, for no reason that Parshall could discern.

So they'd have to do their breaking and entering in the middle of the day, while the lady of the house was lunching.

The next day they used the phone tracker to determine when the bus would pick her up. They hung back behind some trees until they watched her get on the bus.

They sneaked up to the front door, hoping no one saw. Dempsey had learned as a child to pick locks, so it didn't take them more than a minute to get in.

Parshall led them through the formal front room, into the maps room. Locked filing cabinets lined the walls. The Jacksonville Soulpusher Society had not gone digital.

Yvonne looked around, then back at Parshall. "Any idea where to start?" she asked.

Parshall thought for a moment. "I went to the Council because of the Byres family. Let's start with them."

No files with that name. Parshall paused for another moment.

"Let's look for people surrounding the Byres family."

The files weren't categorized by years or events, so they had to look at each one. Parshall started with the As, Dempsey in the middle, and Yvonne with the Zs. One name caught Yvonne's eye: "Zearott." It was an unusual name, and she happened to notice the word "infant." She looked at the year. The file had been created 17 years prior, after the birth and death of a baby girl named Annalisa Zearott. This had been the same day David was born...in the same hospital.

She looked up at the other two. "Halt the presses."

"You think this is it?" Dempsey asked.

"Methinks it is. Let's keep looking, though."

Parshall started looking up at the maps. An uneasy feeling settled in her stomach. The maps were of different sections of Jacksonville. The suburban Southside area was the newest map. There was a big check mark on that one. The older maps, such as those for San Marco and Riverside, had dozens of question marks, check marks and Xs crossed out. The only words left were not favorable, and were probably written after excessive nights of happy hours. She showed the rest of the crew.

"I think we need to visit those places. Agreed?" Yvonne asked.

"Oh, most definitely," Parshall answered.

Something on the messy desk caught Dempsey's attention. He'd recognize the familiar shape of a stylus anywhere.

"You've gotta be kidding me! I didn't know another one of those existed!"

He bolted over and scooped the 20-year-old personal digital assistant off the desk. He looked slyly over at the other two. "I'm guessing you folks don't know how to work this thing, huh?"

"I don't even know what that thing is," answered Yvonne.

"It's the reason I almost got kicked out of science camp!"

Yvonne looked dubious.

"OK, it's *one* of the reasons I almost got kicked out of science camp."

Parshall didn't see an end to their little verbal sparring match, so she interrupted. "What is that, and why is it significant?"

Dempsey smiled. "It's what old folks used before smartphones."

Parshall frowned.

Dempsey started protesting. "OK, OK! I don't need more enemies. *Older people*. It's what people used to have to keep track of meetings and notes. This is Laura's! I can't believe she still has one. This has to be older than us." He said this while looking at Yvonne. Parshall frowned harder.

"Well, let's see what she's been up to," Yvonne encouraged, before Parshall had a chance to find out if the stylus could be used as a weapon.

The only items were a few drink recipes and a personal calendar. There were only two dates marked on the calendar: one for a dentist appointment, and one for a meeting. The meeting was titled "Dirtbags." They all looked at each other.

"The Council?" Parshall asked.

Yvonne and Dempsey slowly nodded their heads.

"But where?" Yvonne asked. "Here?"

Dempsey shook his head. "I don't think so. We haven't seen anyone else enter since we've been watching this place. I think the other pushers avoid this location. I bet it'll be somewhere neutral."

"How are we gonna find it, though?" Yvonne asked, impatiently. "We can't just wait around for her to leave."

Dempsey shrugged. "It worked once before."

"How do you think they communicate? Do they have an online forum? Text messaging group?" Yvonne continued.

"I don't know. Laura doesn't look like the instant messaging or chatting type. She doesn't have a computer here." Dempsey laid back against the wall, frustrated.

Parshall narrowed her eyes. "Laura only goes one place consistently," she began.

"Yeah," the other two answered immediately.

"What does that place have to offer the Council?"

They thought for a second. Food, drink, desserts, tables, chairs, bathrooms...

She gave them a moment more, and then rolled her eyes. "Reach. That restaurant is part of a local chain, with locations all over Jax, including the neighborhoods with all of those question marks and Xs. I bet they have a bulletin board or something. We could check out one of the other locations."

Rothra

Renna was putting the final touches on a flyer for their upcoming performance. She wasn't a graphic artist by any stretch of the imagination, but she'd learned to use the software, and they had a stock photo account.

She wasn't able to concentrate because Andrew was stomping around upstairs in his bedroom. She wanted so badly for him to be a successful, professional musician, but mainly so that he could get his own apartment after graduation.

He hated her calling him Andrew. She mostly did it 'cause it was his name, but also a little bit 'cause she thought he was being pretentious. What's with calling himself Herb? Maybe he'll go through another phase and call himself Herbie.

His payback to her was making up his own nickname for her. This made Renna worry even more for him and his future. He couldn't even find an original retaliation.

She could hear him stomping down the stairs.

"Hey, Rothra. Have you thought about lunch any?"

She sighed. Their parents were visiting relatives in Gainesville. The freezer was stocked with pizzas, chicken bites, and whatever else would appeal to 16-year-olds. She and her brother usually had a staring contest to determine who would turn on the oven and insert the frozen food.

She didn't feel like dealing with any of it. "I'm busy working on your band's advertising. You can put a pizza in the oven."

He frowned. "I don't like this new defiant attitude you've developed."

She didn't even look up. "Yeah, well I don't like trying to resize this stupid picture. For some reason it keeps flipping back to 365 pixels."

He shrugged and headed toward the oven. "Have you been to visit David lately?"

Renna paused, hand on the mouse. She hadn't been since that incident.

She looked up at Andrew. "Something weird happened the last time I was there." She stopped, not sure how to say it without sounding ridiculous. There was no way. "Things in the room started moving. I felt his presence."

He relaxed a little. "Ok, so I'm not the only one. That was weird, huh?"

Another One

"What do you mean there's another one? Another comatose person? Do you think it's the same thing...I mean, a soulless person?"

The nurse didn't like this categorization. Sure, she knew her patient's soul was elsewhere, but she didn't like him being referred to as "soulless."

She backed away from Zoe, and towards her patient. "You know, it's probably not the same thing. His soul is probably perfectly intact. Besides, you'd know if there was another person here without a soul, right?"

Zoe started to nod, then shrugged, looking down. "I don't know what I'd know."

They stood in awkward silence for a few more seconds, until Zoe walked away in confusion.

———— • — • ————

She called Jack. The nurse had shut her out, and despite her repeated viewing of the show *Charmed* over the last few months, Zoe did not know how to scry for the young man's soul.

They met at a coffee shop, which was such a cliche, Zoe thought. She got it, though. Jack wanted to meet in public, and two espressos—though not cheap—were less expensive than two meals.

They sat in the back, Jack against the wall looking out into the restaurant. He insisted that they look down whenever they spoke, to keep onlookers from reading their lips.

"Really?" Zoe asked.

"Really. Not trying to sound arrogant, but I have a lot of enemies. Some are rival investigators who want to know what I know. Some want to stop me. There might even be a few Council sympathizers out there. We don't want to give them any more information than they already have."

"Ok," she agreed. "So what's the plan?"

"This is just an informal meeting..."

Zoe rolled her eyes.

Jack narrowed his. "You give me an idea of what you know, and I'll do the same."

She shrugged. "There's not much for me to tell. I just got dumped into this world a few months ago."

He started mulling something over. "I wonder why your power just woke up. Your parents didn't tell you anything?"

He didn't ask, so she didn't mention that she had just met her mother. "I think my mom's scared. I don't think Laura is what freaked her out—more like what she represents. I think something else about the Council terrifies my family."

"You know I broke into the Council once..." he started, waiting for Zoe's look of surprise and admiration.

"How would I know that? I just met you."

His grin faded a bit. "That was rhetorical. You were supposed to say 'No! I didn't know that! Tell me more!'"

She sighed. "I really don't get people."

It was his turn to sigh. "The moment's ruined. Anyway, it wasn't easy to break into the Council. The administrator works odd hours. However, I eventually figured out that she goes to lunch at the same time every day. I found out because I happened to show up where she was. I had been getting frustrated and needed a break."

Zoe didn't look too impressed, especially since he'd just admitted that he'd stumbled onto his big opportunity.

"So, anyways, I'm going to show you what I got. But, I don't want to bring my research out in public. I'd like to go back to my apartment to look at it."

"I just met you. I'm not going back to your apartment with you."

"No! Not like that! I'm more than twice your age." He stopped for a moment, calculating...slowly. "Sixteen times two is thirty-two," he whispered, under his breath. "Actually, I'm two and half times your age. So chillax, I'm harmless."

"First of all: There is no 'harmless' when a forty-year-old man is talking to a minor he doesn't know. Second of all: 'Chillax?' Did you grow up in a surf shop? *Dumb and Dumber* called. They want their dialogue back."

"You know, that's pretty dated, too—that 'So and so called, they want their whatever back.'"

"Yeah," she agreed, reluctantly. "I've been watching a lot of 90's shows on T.V."

He nodded. "I have a lot of down time, too."

"Still," she continued, unwavering. "I don't know you. Therefore, we're meeting in public."

He had to admit that was pretty smart of her. He knew he wasn't a threat, but she didn't know that.

"I've got an idea," Zoe said. "I need to go shopping. Do you think the Gestapo would follow you to a shopping center?"

"You know...you remind me of the woman I'm dating. She has the same irreverent way of speaking."

———— • ——— • ————

"I've never thought much about fashion. Not my fashion, anyway. I don't even know what size I am."

Jack was starting to think he'd dodged a bullet by not having children.

"Am I the bad girl type? Black jeans and a leather jacket?"

He followed her as she pulled out pieces of clothing from each rack.

"You're right," she answered, despite not receiving any feedback. "It's too hot for a leather jacket. Besides, my sisters only gave me a few hundred dollars to spend."

She pulled out a black t-shirt featuring a sangria glass crafted together by dark pink sequins.

"I know I'm not old enough to drink, so I shouldn't be wearing a sangria glass, but I want something like this."

Jack ignored Zoe's great conflict in favor of getting actual business done. "Look, I scanned all of these documents onto an SD card. Against my better judgment, I'm going to show you these slides as you go around being bedazzled by shiny t-shirts."

She looked annoyed. "I've never gotten to wear shiny anything before. This is an exciting day for me."

"It should be exciting because you might finally get some of the answers you've been looking for."

"Fine, Mr. All Business and No Play. Whatcha got?"

He swiped his phone to an image of a newspaper article. It was about a local trial lawyer falling to his death years before.

"The article makes it seem like suicide. Well, that's probably what everyone thought. Lawyer's overwhelmed by big case and jumps off bridge. But I looked into it. What the article doesn't mention is that he was winning his case. The defendant was going to get off. However..." He swiped the screen to make the print larger. "Look toward the end of the article. A bystander reported that someone came up to the lawyer right before he fell. The person did an upward motion with his hands, and the lawyer's body went limp. The article doesn't expound on this, but I think whatever the man did with his hands caused enough of a wave to send the lawyer's body over."

Zoe dropped the cherry-colored baby tee she'd been fondling. "No kidding? That's it! That's exactly what happens! The Soulpusher pushes the soul up with her or his hands. In this case, though, it doesn't sound like the person was dead yet. If the soul didn't go upwards, then I don't know where it would be."

She didn't voice her next thought. *Or, maybe the soul went into the bystander.*

"Could it still be at the bridge?" Jack asked.

She shuddered. "If that's the case, then we have to help him."

San Marco

Yvonne and Parshall waited to be seated, while Dempsey went to check out the attached store, in case there were clues.

"My little vacation will be over soon. The nurse who was working for me is gone. Her patient went back home."

"When do you go back to work?"

"In a few days."

Yvonne changed the subject. "What if there are no clues? Maybe the Council person comes in and they just know to tell her or him where the meeting is."

"Well, in that case we're screwed. We have to try, though."

Their server seated them near the window. They looked around for clues while they waited for Dempsey to get back. Parshall started with the draft beer menu, which was pretty straight forward. The usual domestic brands plus a few locals. The import menu was good, which Parshall expected from a European-type bistro.

They were both startled by the server, who, in her defense, was just doing her job.

"Have you decided yet?"

"How often does the beer menu change?"

Justifiably, the server looked like she thought that was an odd question. "Seasonally, though once in a while we'll get something new, and change out something else for it."

"Once in a while? Like once a month?"

The server paused before she spoke, undoubtedly trying to shake the annoyance out of her voice. "There isn't a set schedule. It's just whenever the buyer gets something new. It could be in two months or three weeks."

Parshall decided to rest her line of questioning. She was starting to think the clue wouldn't be in the beer.

The server turned to Yvonne. "Do you know what you'd like?"

Yvonne pretended to glance over the menu. Parshall could tell she was pretending because her eyes kept slipping over to the chalkboard with specials.

"I can't read that from over here. What does it say?"

This time the server laid out a heavy sigh, but coughed over it. "Cuban on rye with chips."

"How often does that change?"

"Oh my...I don't know." She thought for a few seconds. "It changes every week. I have Mondays off, but it's always different when I come in on Tuesday."

Yvonne stretched out a "hmmm..." for a lot longer than most people would. "I can't decide. What's good for the soul?" she asked, acting on a hunch.

The server clutched her notepad to her chest like it was the only thing between her and crazy, because it was. "I'm sorry?" she asked, hoping the young woman would just order an actual menu item instead of turning it into a riddle.

"... good for the soul?" Yvonne sputtered, not wanting to admit that her hunch was off.

"We have soup."

"What kind?"

"French onion."

"Ok. I'll have that."

The server turned to Parshall, but she quickly asked for a few more minutes.

Parshall began laughing as soon as the server was out of sight. "Did you solve the mystery? Does the French onion soup mean the Council is meeting in France?"

Yvonne frowned, giving Parshall a low "hmph."

"Well, you've got your choice of meeting places in that beer menu," Yvonne countered. "Do you think the meeting's in Holland? Or Latvia?"

Parshall looked down at the beer menu again. "Latvia's on here? Cool!"

———— • ———— • ————

Dempsey went up to the counter, various pieces of chocolate in his mouth. The cashier looked suspiciously at him. "You know you gotta pay for those, right?"

"Do you have fortune cookies?" Dempsey asked, not even registering that the man had spoken.

"No, but your future is going to involve jail, if you don't pay for those chocolates."

Dempsey dug out some dollar bills and pushed them toward the cashier.

———— • ———— • ————

Yvonne and Parshall were arguing when Dempsey got back to the table.

"Why are you all stressing so much?" he asked, sitting down.

Parshall sat back in her chair while Yvonne answered. "We're just out of ideas. Nothing we've thought of has panned out. Did you get anything in the shop?"

"Raspberry chocolate is good. So is orange chocolate, surprisingly. Nothing on the bulletin board that you wouldn't see at the local coffee shop."

"Maybe we'll try the bathrooms later," Yvonne said.

None of them had been paying attention to the music. The lunch crowd babble had been overpowering the sound of the speakers. A song pierced through the jibber jabber of the neighboring tables.

"Oh, this song is giving me a headache," Yvonne said, putting her hands up to her ears.

Parshall raised her eyebrows. "Elvis gives you a headache?"

"Not all of it. Just this song, so far. I could use a little less of his conversation right now."

"You're an American anomaly, Yvonne." She paused for a second. "Come to think of it, wasn't 'Can't Help Falling in Love with You' on when we came in?"

She waved over the server, who looked exasperated.

"Are you ready to order?"

"Grilled cheese sandwich and chips. Have you been playing Elvis all day?"

"All week. I know he's the King, but c'mon...I have to listen to it all day. Do they even make blue suede shoes?"

"You can't change it?" Yvonne asked.

"No. The first week of every month the owner sets the station. We're forbidden from touching it until the 8th of the month. It's a fireable offense."

"Huh..." Parshall sat back in her chair again, thinking. "What was it last month?"

She sighed the sigh of someone with a heavy burden. "The Beach Boys. I never liked them much to begin with, but a whole week? I was ready to quit." She looked at Dempsey, who she'd just realized was there. "Do you know what you want?"

He was startled by the question. Yvonne nudged him and pointed to the menu. He nodded back to her.

"He'll take a grilled cheese sandwich. Can I have one, too? Soup won't be enough."

The server happily walked away. Parshall broke out into a broad grin.

"Well, I think we got our clue." she said.

Yvonne smiled, too. "Yeah, but what does it mean?"

"Well, I think Beach Boys last month meant Beach Boulevard. I'm thinking close to the actual beach. What about Elvis Presley, though?"

They all just stared at each other for a minute. "She called him the King, right?" Yvonne asked.

"Yeah."

"Do you think it could be King Street in Riverside?"

"Genius, Yvonne! Yes! But where on King Street?"

"Well, most of those places are restaurants. We'd be looking for a place a little more private, right?"

"I'd think," Yvonne agreed. "We know what time the meeting starts. We could just go there and look for a bunch of people entering a building."

"Sounds like a plan to me," Dempsey said, as he sucked water through a straw.

King Street

The three convened in front of the Baptist church. "Dempsey, why don't you take the area near the comic book shop," Parshall said.

Yvonne protested. "What? You think because he's a boy he likes comics, and I don't?"

Parshall rolled her eyes. "I think that since he's a young man, he'll blend in more with the comic book crowd. I'm just trying to make the smartest decisions."

Yvonne crossed her arms. "Where do I go?"

"I'm going up toward the warehouses. I want you to stay where the foot traffic is heavy—in front of a restaurant. You look older, but you're not. I don't want you near the pubs."

"Yes, ma'am," Yvonne answered.

———— • ———— • ————

Turned out Dempsey picked the figurative lucky straw. He recognized Laura's old car rumbling down the road. He watched as she pulled into a space in front of an empty former restaurant. It was small, probably barely big enough to seat ten people. Luckily, it was at the end of the small shopping center, so there were windows around the side.

He texted the other two, advising them to take the back way, away from the storefront.

Parshall, Dempsey and Yvonne sneaked around to the back of the building, out of sight of the late-night churchgoers and wandering comic book enthusiasts. They peeped over the windowsill and looked in. They could see a long conference table with people sitting around it. Each person had a card in front of them. Altmeyer's card was stained with what was either blood or red wine, but it looked to read Arlington.

The other card titles were also names of Jacksonville subsections. Yvonne had only been there a week, but she recognized some of the names: San Marco, Riverside, Downtown, Northside, Westside and Southside. There were a few others she hadn't heard of.

"What's East?" she asked Parshall.

"That's the name the suburbanites toward the Intracoastal gave themselves. They're between Beach, Atlantic and Turner Boulevards, going toward the ocean."

"There's no one sitting there," Dempsey observed, though they could all three plainly see that.

Inside, Southside spoke up. "Where's East?"

Riverside answered. "Probably stuck in the salon."

San Marco shushed her. "Don't be so judgmental."

"You definitely can't judge," Riverside replied. "You'd be late if your salon weren't just across the river."

San Marco frowned. "At least our parks aren't splattered with duck poop."

"What parks? You mean those medians you call parks? You put a piece of ground in between two roads, and that's a park?"

"Ladies and gentlemen," Laura bellowed. "Let's get started. East can catch up later. No doubt she'll hear the gossip from Southside, anyway."

She cleared her throat, wanting to stall. This wasn't going to be an easy discussion.

"You know why we're here," Laura started. "We've been asked to intervene in a civic matter by one of our generous donors."

Everyone groaned. Northside spoke. "Laura, we've had this discussion dozens of times. That part of our history is done. Over. I don't care how much money or resources we get, we are not in the business of pushing souls anywhere but Heaven. Haven't you heard of Karma?"

"Tandie," Laura began, addressing Northside by her name. "Our mothers go way back."

Tandie huffed. "Our mothers go way back because my mother was assigned to look after your mother. Even back then we knew your family couldn't be trusted."

Westside interrupted. "The last time we did that was twenty years ago, and it tore the Council apart. We maneuvered a soul, and we ruined a family. We are not doing that again."

Parshall, Yvonne and Dempsey held their gasps in, but glanced quickly at each other, wondering if each was thinking the same thing. Twenty years ago? David was only sixteen. Who did they harm twenty years ago?"

"Do we even know if anyone can still do it? Has anyone tried?" Springfield asked.

Englewood, a quiet, small gentleman, raised his hand. "I tried once. I just managed to displace the soul. I had to work extra hard to get him where he was supposed to go."

Laura looked downcast. "I can't do it, either."

"When did you try?" Springfield asked.

"A few weeks ago. In the restaurant I go to. This woman would not shut up. She didn't like the clam chowder, there wasn't enough wine in her glass, her potato salad was too potato-y. She wasn't happy with anything. Anyway, I figured maybe she could ride shotgun with the waiter for a while."

Everyone fell into silence.

"Well, it didn't work! I would have put her back, anyway."

"Not without doing a ton of harm," San Marco warned.

"So," Southside interjected. "We don't know anyone who can do it. Why are we talking about this, then?"

"Because," Laura said. "I think I know of someone who can."

The window gang looked at each other again, mouths hanging open. "David," Yvonne whispered.

The other two nodded.

A car screeched up to the front door, not concerned that it wasn't a parking space. Dempsey scurried to the corner in time to see a tanned, high-heeled woman rushing out of the driver's seat and power walking inside.

Dempsey scurried back, trying not to make any noise. Parshall and Yvonne had crouched down below the window, so the woman walking in wouldn't see them. They stayed there, despite not being able to see the Council members anymore. They had an idea of who was saying what.

"Where were you?" Southside asked.

"Basking in the sun?" Riverside asked.

"No," a voice answered, the person out-of-breath. "I had to do an emergency soul-section. We need more people!"

The room erupted—a dozen voices clamoring to be heard. One voice bulldozed the others.

"You know why we don't have more people. More people means more interference," Laura asserted.

"We don't do that stuff anymore! We don't have to worry about interference."

"Have you been listening? I *want* to do that 'stuff' again. We need money. You don't have to see the property tax bills, the repair bills. You don't see the dwindling bank account. Do you think all the wheels get greased with aloe leaves? No. It's with money, and we don't have any."

The room was silent again.

"That's what I thought. You go take time to discuss it with your people. I'm ordering another meeting. One week from today."

Riverside spoke up. "Do you want to meet here next week? Same time?"

Laura replied. "OK, but Tandie..." The gang could hear her voice change direction. "...you wanted to host the next official meeting, right?

"Yeah. There's an old Golden Corral I can get. We can enter from the back. I still have to confirm, though, so we probably want to play the music game."

Everyone groaned.

"Any ideas?" Westside asked. "I don't want another guessing game like last month. You know how long Beach Boulevard is."

"I thought you'd figure out 'Beach,' like toward the beach," East said.

"How am I supposed to know that?"

Riverside took over the conversation. "So any thoughts on music?"

Tandie answered. "Well, corral sounds like a cowboy thing. You want Western music?"

The noise hit another high. "The staff will quit if we make them listen to "Home on the Range" for a solid week," Westside protested.

Tandie frowned. "I'm sure that's not the only Western song. But, okay. How about choral music?"

"We'll just put the staff to sleep," East answered.

No one liked her joke.

"Okay, I'm sorry," East continued. "You all have lovely voices, and I apologize that I intentionally missed every single performance."

Riverside huffed. "I have recordings. We can use those."

"Oh, Lord," East retorted.

Laura corralled them all up. "Next week. Same time, same day, same location."

The investigators stayed still, listening to the sound of chairs scraping across tile.

The Lawyer

Jack pulled into a parking lot a block down from the lawyer's office, not wanting anyone to see his car. He and Zoe got out of the car and walked down to the small gray building.

When they walked in, a chime hanging from the door clattered. The reception area was reminiscent of a doctor's office, except the magazines on the table weren't about health. They were mostly law and science journals. A woman in her 50's came in from the hallway and extended her hand.

"I'm Sheila. How may I help you?"

Zoe took her hand first. She'd actually never shaken anyone's hand. It was weird. "Is this the law firm that handled the Shepherd case a few decades ago?"

Sheila slid her hand out of Zoe's. "Yes, but that was a long time ago. Why are you asking about that?"

Zoe looked uneasily at Jack. She wasn't sure what to say. He wasn't either.

"We're amateur detectives," he ventured. There was no point in pretending to be real detectives. They'd be busted as soon as she got to her computer. "We're looking at old cases that we think should have gone differently."

"Well, that's a hornet's nest. I hope you brought protective gear. Yes, this is the firm, but I wasn't the lawyer."

"We know the lawyer is deceased, but we were wondering if you knew him. If you know anything about the case," Jack said.

She glared at him. "I know everything about that case. That case got my boss killed. I was his paralegal at the time."

Zoe looked up at the diplomas on the wall. They were a few decades old. "Why were you a paralegal when you had a law degree?"

She pursed her lips. "What does that have to do with anything?"

"Nothing," Zoe answered.

The lawyer shrugged. "I didn't pass the dang bar exam. Apparently that's normal—not passing the exam on the first try. But I didn't know that, so I felt defeated. When he died, though, I started thinking maybe I was only hurting myself by not trying again. Also, he willed the practice to me, and I wasn't about to let another lawyer take over."

"He didn't have family?" Jack asked.

"No. His parents were already gone, and no siblings. No husband, either. He said he'd never found the right man."

Zoe and Jack looked at her, each poised to say something, but not sure what that something would be.

"Oh! I get it!" Zoe exclaimed.

"Were you interested in him?" Jack asked.

She smiled slyly. "If she were here, I'd introduce you to my wife. She does the accounting and scheduling."

It was Jack's turn to be thrown off. "So you're married to a woman?"

Sheila rolled her eyes hard. Zoe felt embarrassed for Jack.

Sheila stared at the strange young woman. "So, what kind of detectives did y'all say you were? Obviously not good ones."

Busted, Zoe thought.

Jack shook his head in protest, then realized she was right, and stopped.

"I'm sorry," he started. "I didn't realize you were—"

"Gay? How could you know? I'm not wearing my gay jumpsuit."

"No," Jack stumbled. "I know plenty of gay people. It's just that I already knew they were gay. I mean, I knew they were gay before I met them."

"Oh, I apologize. Is there some sort of vetting process I missed?"

"No, no, no. I mean...I'm not very articulate."

"Obviously."

"Ma'am?" Zoe asked, hoping to steer the conversation back. "I think we need to start over. My colleague and I are idiots. We don't know how to deal with people. I've been in a coma for most of my life, and he...well, he deals with ghosts."

Ten minutes later they were sitting in her office. Though Jack wasn't literally "in the doghouse," he *was* sitting *on* a doghouse.

"My Yorkie Champagne has a delicate stomach and one of my clients thought it would be cute to give her some of his sandwich. Therefore, I have to get the vomit removed from my second guest chair."

She looked over at Jack picking champagne-colored hairs off of his pants. "I have a cushion, if that helps with the comfort level."

Jack shook his head. He didn't want to antagonize Sheila anymore.

"What can you tell us about your boss?" he asked.

"He was a great lawyer. I'm not just saying that because I worked for him. His instincts were spot-on, and he was known for selecting clients who actually turned out to be honorable. He was a bit of a detective himself." She looked over at Jack, shifting on the wooden platform. "Probably a better one than you. He could see how the evidence was misleading the police."

"Do you think the police could have had anything to do with it?"

She shook her head. "Nah. He'd been doing this for years. He was well known to the police. It was almost like a friendly rivalry. If they saw him snooping into a case, they knew it was time to up their game."

"Do you think it's possible his instinct failed him that time? Maybe the guy was guilty?" Jack asked.

"No. He was winning the case. Why would the defendant kill him? He was the client's best chance. Whoever killed my boss wanted our client to go to jail."

Zoe thought for a moment. "That makes sense. They wanted to be sure he went to trial and lost."

"Yup. And that's what happened. The man is still in jail for supposedly killing his neighbor."

"What was the contradictory evidence your boss found?"

Her expression softened. "I don't know. Usually he shared his thoughts with me, but he kept this one totally under wraps—this case really had him paranoid. I've been trying to figure it out for years. Maybe I'm the one who's not a good detective."

• ——— • ———

Zoe and Jack walked back to the car. "So?" Jack asked.

"We go to the bridge and I try to find him."

They got in the car. Before he started the engine, he looked over at Zoe. "After this, do you think you'll feel comfortable trying to wake him up?"

They hadn't talked about "the boy at the hospital" since they had first met. Whatever Zoe did with the soul on the bridge was going to be her first attempt at purposefully moving a soul. Would she be successful? Would she be able to do it for a living person?

"I'll try."

Jack drove slowly toward the bridge. Cars honked behind them and swerved around. He wasn't in a hurry to get to their destination. In fact, he had to resist the urge to turn around, drop Zoe off wherever she lived, and go back to his one-bedroom apartment.

It had gotten dark in the few minutes traveling between the lawyer's office and the river. Jack parked in a lot near the bridge and they both got out.

Zoe gasped as they approached the entrance. She looked through the fog that was rising from the water and up through the grates. Hundreds of gray, blurry figures wafted up and down the walkway. Some wandered into traffic, but weren't affected by the oncoming cars.

She tried to make out faces, but the features blurred together. She'd seen a picture of the lawyer standing on a yacht, so she had an idea of what to look for. She finally spotted him standing near the railing, looking out over the water. *Probably looking for his body,* she thought.

She turned around and gestured for Jack to stay back. He reflexively moved toward her. As long as she was a minor, she was his responsibility. Her hand shot out and the energy from that gesture stopped him in his tracks.

Zoe waded through the narrow stream of misty figures. The women and men were dressed in styles from the 1940's to present day. There were probably even older spirits down in the water, from before there was a bridge. Maybe they were guiding long-gone boats down the river, or rehashing the same Sunday outing over and over. She didn't look down to find out.

She approached the man in the gray suit, and got as far as she could without him dissipating. She could feel what passed for breath coming from him. He turned to her. The wind blew his short sandy hair.

"Am I dead?" he asked, his gray eyes misting.

"Yes," she said. "I'm going to try to help you."

He looked back out to the light cast down on the river.

"I'd like to go wherever Gary is."

"Who's Gary?"

He looked down. "My boyfriend. He died several years ago. I haven't known what to do since. Everything I did was for him, even the law practice. He was the smarter of us two. I figured I'd just answer the phones while he became the superstar."

Zoe smiled. "I think there's a good chance you'll see him. I need to talk to you about the case you're working on." She was careful to use the present tense.

He nodded. "I need to go home and work on it. Jury selection starts in a few days."

She didn't have the heart to tell him that the jury had come and gone.

"Your assistant is going to work on that. You just need to let me know all the evidence."

"Oh, well that's easy. There's certainly reasonable doubt. Neighbors saw my client go up to the door and bang on it. But, they also saw him leave. When the police found the body, they also found a trail of footprints leading away from the back. The common thinking was that my client had circled around and gone into the house through the back door. It had rained heavily the night before, so most of the footprints had washed away. The only ones left stopped about three feet from the door. It was hard to determine where those prints came from or where they went."

He fumbled around where the pockets of his pants had once been. "However, I took pictures of one faint print that was closer to the woods behind the house. It was pointing *toward* the building. If my client had circled around from the front, that footprint would have been angled differently, and wouldn't have been so near the woods. I also took pictures of broken branches where it looked like someone had walked through."

Zoe was elated. They were closer to solving this man's mystery...though they weren't much closer to figuring out who killed him.

"Where are the pictures?" she asked.

He smiled. "I've got rolls of film back at my office."

Her smile faded. "Rolls of...twenty-year-old film?"

"Has it been that long?"

Zoe changed tactics. "Do you know who would want your client to go to jail?"

"I guess the person who really murdered the victim."

Zoe sighed. "You're not being very helpful. Do you have any idea who pushed you?"

He looked around. Zoe hadn't realized until then, but all of the spirits on the bridge were swarming around them. She supposed they were looking for a way out. She supposed she had to give it to them. *Were all the other Soulpushers averse to bridges?*

"It was dark. Misty...like now. I felt a push and then I was here, standing on this bridge, but my body wasn't." He looked down. "It was there," he said, pointing to the waves below.

"Fan freakin' tastic," Zoe said. "Thank you."

She gestured for all of the spirits to circle around her. They began rotating like a slow, sluggish tornado. She raised her hands and pushed them up. Collectively, they all rose toward a fixed point in the sky. Within a few seconds they were all gone. It was eerily quiet on the bridge after that.

———— • ———— • ————

Jack dropped Zoe off at the coffee shop where her bicycle was. She wasn't quite ready to tell him where she lived, though he seemed like a good guy. She was, however, prepared to accept his offer of money for a rideshare. The hard part was finding a car that could accommodate her bicycle. An hour later an SUV with a bike rack and a Salt Life sticker showed up.

When she got home, her mother was still up. Zoe smiled at her, but the smile was not reciprocated.

"Will you sit with me here a few minutes, Zoe?"

This worried her. In the few months she'd known her mother, she had never used her preferred name. She'd always called her Annalisa—as if that really were her name, and not just a label her abandoned body had been given.

"I'd like to try to make you understand what happened sixteen years ago."

Zoe didn't like where this was going. She was finally starting to feel okay about her situation. She considered running back to her room, to the bed her body had known for so long.

Then again, maybe what her mother told her would give her some clarity. Explain why she had to "grow up" as a secondary character in David's life.

She looked at her mother's face and it clicked. She had seen her at the skatepark, the soccer field, and the jazz band performances. She'd figured she had a kid at the school. Well, she had, but the kid didn't play soccer or guitar.

"I know you have a lot of questions about why I did what I did. Believe me, not a day has gone by that I didn't resent having to do it. Truth is, I didn't have a choice. They would have found you and kicked your spirit upstairs. Your body would have faded, and then died. By me putting your spirit into that boy's body, you got to live. It wasn't the ideal existence, but I couldn't kill you. And that's what they wanted. They wanted me to kill you."

She got quiet and looked at the wall. Zoe didn't know what to say, so she looked at the wall, too.

"I know that you've been looking into our...whatever you'd call it...'chapter.' You've figured out that we do things differently than other Soulpushers. We're only allowed two kids, and those kids have to stay and work close to areas of high death probability."

"Why?" Zoe asked.

"We were told the magic is sparse, and there's not enough for a large family. Because of this, there aren't enough Soulpushers in Jacksonville, so we have to be regulated. We work at hospitals because that's where most deaths occur. We work as cops because maybe we can get to the crime scene in time. It kind of makes sense, though I always thought there had to be a better way."

She shifted more toward Zoe and looked her directly in the eye.

"After I gave birth to you, I was left with a choice, and I had to act quickly. I was supposed to guide your spirit up to the afterlife. As far as most Soulpushers know, it's a one-direction ticket. We push souls up, not out.

But in that moment I did something different. I pretended that my power was a baseball bat, and I smacked your soul to the left, away from the light. I didn't know what I was doing. I could have killed you, for all I knew, but I took the chance."

She put her hand on Zoe's shoulder. Zoe backed away, her eyes flickering between confusion and pain. Her mother was not deterred.

"I figured out that night that I could do something incredible—I could control souls."

Zoe narrowed her eyes and crossed her arms. "Mom, that's what you do—control souls."

Her mother may have missed most of this daughter's upbringing, but she'd seen that gesture from her other children. It conveyed the big three: condescension, amusement and disbelief, or CAD as she called it. Her daughter was definitely being a cad.

"It *seems* like we control souls, but we don't. Like I said—it's a one-directional trip. We send souls up. We don't send them over. This was something new and intoxicating."

Mrs. Zearott—hating her paranoia, and feeling foolish because of it—got up and turned on the TV so that the sound would drown out her talking.

"That's when I started to think that maybe I wasn't the first. Maybe the Council knew all about this, and that's why they have such a tight leash on us. They don't want the rank-and-file to know what they're doing. So they winnow down the population until there's a shortage, and dozens of deaths go by untended. That's their test ground. They know they have no pushers in certain locations, so they're free to stalk those areas."

She paused. "They isolate you so that you don't feel connected. When you're not connected, you shield yourself from people. Without those relationships, you have no reason to take risks. You're not like that, though. You're incredibly open, and incredibly capable. Plus, the Council doesn't know you exist. You can work in secret."

"Um...OK?" Zoe finally answered, not sure she felt the same confidence as her mother.

Her mom smiled. "Please don't think I like this one bit. You're my daughter. I don't want you out there getting hurt or worse. But..." She folded her arms in defiance, just as Zoe had done a few minutes earlier. "...I know you've been researching us. You've been meeting with the nurse and that occultist. You've already put yourself out there. I just want you to understand who you're up against, and what they're doing."

"Huh." Zoe looked down. "So you really think I can do this?"

"Did that boy ever show you Star Wars?"

Zoe nodded.

Her mother smiled wryly. "You're our only hope."

The Hospital

Renna and Herb sat in the hospital room, talking quietly to each other, and occasionally to David. There wasn't much to say except that the band was still practicing, and that school was the same.

David lay completely still. Not a sneeze, not a cough, not even the restlessness that came with most people's sleep.

Renna turned toward her brother. "I felt something here a few days ago."

Herb was still looking at David's placid face. "Did you feel his presence?"

"Yeah!" She was surprised, having never heard Andrew talk about anything that didn't relate to...well, himself.

"I've felt it too. What do you think it means?"

"I think it means his soul is here. You know who knows a lot about souls?"

Herb's smile didn't make it past a smirk. "Grandmother talks a lot about souls. She also claims to see them and talk to them. I'm not sure we want her brand of eccentricity here right now."

"You sure are mean."

"...truthful."

"I want to call her."

"Okay" he said, fishing out his phone. "You get to explain to Mrs. Byres why a loud stranger wearing a rainbow of colors has descended upon her son."

———— • ———— • ————

Zoe spotted Jack's car in the parking lot immediately. She shook her head at his car. The windows were taped up in some spots, and the paint had more scratches than a klutz in a furniture shop. She would know because she'd discovered that she was klutz, and she and her sisters had recently gone furniture shopping.

Jack was on the phone when Zoe got in his car. She couldn't hear who he was talking to because he used one of those hands-free wireless ear plugs. David hated those things because he always thought the person was talking to him. She had to admit she hated them, too. Whatever happened to saying hello to the person who gets in your car? She'd only been a full person for a few months, and already she was silently lecturing on etiquette.

It sounded like Jack was talking to his girlfriend. He was talking about meeting someone at the hospital. Zoe could tell the other person was annoyed because the earpiece was vibrating due to the volume.

"No, I'm not exploiting your son's situation. I promise, this girl has a bearing on David's situation."

Oh, he was talking about her. Zoe didn't like someone talking about her when she was right there in the car. And what was up with "David"? That wasn't the young man's name.

She started looking out the window...nothing else to do. She saw the familiar cluster of fast-food restaurants, the same geese who walked up and down the little lake shore...no different than the thousands of other times she'd been on that street, except for now she couldn't nestle into her mind hammock. She was the one having to pretend to look alive.

———— • ———— • ————

Yvonne and Dempsey had been staying with Parshall for the past week. Yvonne needed to go back to Gainesville, so they had all agreed to meet at the hospital and talk to David's mother. Parshall was working that day, so the kids took the bus. They hadn't actually met David's mother, so they were a little nervous as they took the elevator up. They were also nervous because they'd be seeing David. They held hands as the elevator went up, and they tightened their grip as the door opened.

Mercedes had gotten into the habit of visiting David on her lunch break. She was so regular that the nurse, Parshall, had started bringing her cafeteria meals. She didn't know if it was being charged to David's room, or if the nurse was just taking the food. She didn't care.

She hadn't gone a day without puffy eyes and balled-up tissues since the whole ordeal had started. One day her son was fine: Going to band practice, going to school...then the next day he didn't wake up. Jack said he thought he knew what was going on. It involved some kind of soothsayer...shaman, or something that started with an "s."

She smiled reflexively as she noticed Herb and Renna. She didn't really feel joy at seeing them—no offense to them—but she didn't feel joy at all. She was grateful to them for not abandoning him, and for watching over him, but they were also a reminder that teenage life had moved on without him.

She put her purse beside the third chair in the room and sat down. She'd stopped asking if there had been any change. She'd stopped asking how they were doing, how their parents were, or how the band was. She just sat there and looked at David.

The nurse came in with the tray and handed it to Mercedes. She seemed hesitant, like she wanted to ask her something else. Mercedes never needed anything else, so she didn't know what the nurse was waiting for. A tip?

"Ms., er, Mrs. Byres..." She looked over at Renna and Herb. "May I speak to you privately?"

Mercedes frowned. Was it something about David?

"Of course," she answered, looking over at the kids. They got up and left the room.

Parshall kneeled down beside Mercedes. "There isn't an easy way to say this. I belong to an old order of people called Soulpushers."

Mercedes gasped. That had been the word Jack had used.

Parshall continued. "Basically, we're responsible for making sure that departing souls get to the afterlife. That's why I work in a hospital. Lots of departing souls."

Mercedes started crying.

"Lots of incoming souls, too," Parshall interjected. "That's where your son comes in...uh...came in. Two of his friends are at the nurse's station. We've been looking into your son's situation. May I bring them in?"

Mercedes got confused. Two of his friends? Renna and Herb? They were just in here.

"Sure. You can bring whomever you want in here. Give it a few minutes and you'll have another Soulpusher in here."

Parshall started to speak, but didn't know how to respond. She had no idea what other Soulpusher Mrs. Byres was talking about. She went into the hallway and stopped abruptly. The number of teenagers had doubled. Her two teenagers were talking to two other teenagers. The teenagers were multiplying. It was like a horror movie.

———— • ——— • ————

Yvonne and Dempsey looked over at the door that was opening. Parshall was ready for them. They looked at each other. Neither one especially wanted to go in. They weren't fond of the idea of standing near a body that was living, but had no soul.

They looked back over at Renna and Herb, who both looked distraught and tired.

Renna spoke. "We're tired of being left out. We know something's going on. We're his best friends. We need to be in there with him." Herb nodded in agreement.

"C'mon kids," Parshall yelled-whispered. "You're not making this any easier."

All four kids went into the already cramped room. If David's soul was in there, it was probably pushed into a corner.

Yvonne and Dempsey had never seen Mrs. Byres before. She and David looked a lot alike, except Mrs. Byres' face was sallow...like the life had been sucked out. She slumped in the chair next to the bed, holding David's hand. She looked up at the four shapes that had just filtered into the room.

"Hello Renna and Andrew. Hello children I don't know." Mercedes' voice was robotic, and only part of her was aware she'd even spoken.

"We know your son from science camp," Yvonne began. "We took chemistry together." She looked over at Dempsey. "Dempsey thought it would be funny to tinker with the science experiment."

Dempsey frowned.

"He almost got us both killed..."

"Are you really still bitter about that?" he interrupted.

She made a face like she had a lemon in her mouth. "Just stating the facts. Anyway, I felt like I was leaving my body, but then I saw something made of light come out of your son's body."

Mercedes made a noise that sounded like something was coming out of *her* body.

"I know how this sounds," Yvonne continued, "but I'm serious. The same thing happened at the lake near Gainesville."

"That was you?" Mercedes asked.

"That was me, and your son saved my life...again. We've been talking to—" She gestured to Parshall, who was in the doorframe "—Ms. Cope, and she has an idea of what's going on."

Parshall walked in, and knelt beside Mercedes.

"We believe that your son was housing another soul...the spirit of a Soulpusher. When the spirit was confronted with a crisis, she unfolded herself from David. My guess is that one time she unfolded from him and he came out with her by accident...like a dryer sheet getting stuck to a piece of clothing."

Mercedes didn't say anything—she just stared coldly at the nurse.

"I'm not saying your son's spirit is a dryer sheet. I was just trying for an analogy..." Parshall looked over at the kids, who shrugged.

"So, anyway, we need to find this spirit. She will be able to ease David's spirit back into his body."

Mrs. Byres vomited onto her lap. Parshall disappeared down the hallway to get some towels. Renna ran into the bathroom to get a paper towel and came back to wipe Mercedes' face. "I'm sorry, Mrs. Byres. I think they're right about David's spirit being out, though.

Mercedes started crying harder. Parshall came back and wiped off her skirt. Renna looked down at Parshall as she put hydrogen peroxide on the stain. Parshall, sensing she was being stared at, looked up.

"Soulpushers are responsible for getting souls up to heaven?" Renna asked.

"Yeah. Heaven, the afterlife, whatever you want to call it."

"...and you do this whenever you see someone dying?"

"Well, it sounds morbid when you say it that way, but yes."

"So...if you pass by a wreck, you insist on stopping and getting out, even though there's nothing you can do to help the person stay alive?"

Parshall frowned. "Well, I'm a nurse, so I *can* help them stay alive. But if I can't help them when they're alive, then I help them transition."

"But you stop anytime you think someone may be dying?"

"Once again, sounds morbid when you say it that way, but yes."

Renna looked over at her brother. "Sounds like anyone you know?"

———— • ———— • ————

Grandma Sheardon drove down I-10. She hated taking the highway...too many fatal accidents. Too many lost souls wandering around. She had two choices: Stop and help every one of them and never make her destination, or fly by, pretending she didn't have a responsibility.

Oh, heck. She couldn't just leave them there. But she'd been practicing a new technique she'd taught herself: Drive-by Soulpushing. It was crass, but it worked.

She saw a formerly living human walking along the side of the road. She checked to make sure no one was beside or behind her. She slowed enough to get a lock on him. She heard the familiar "whoosh" sound as she pushed his soul upwards. She looked back long enough to make sure he connected with the upper realm. Some Soulpushers didn't think their job extended to that, but Regina Sheardon felt a responsibility. If she left before he clicked in heavenly place, he'd smack his way back down to Earth. More years wandering a lonely highway, unless she got him on the way back.

The drive from Tallahassee to Jacksonville was so boring. She didn't know why her son had to settle in Jacksonville. She'd told him they had everything in Tallahassee: Pensacola wasn't too far away, the Gulf was nearby—it wasn't even that long a drive to Tampa. But no...he liked Jacksonville.

The Soulpushers there were closed off...almost cult like. She couldn't tell her son that, though, because she'd never told him she was a Soulpusher. The ability skipped him, so why bother? If he didn't have it, then his children probably wouldn't have it. She chastised herself. Maybe if she'd told her grandchildren, they'd be prepared when confronted with it. Why were they confronted with it, though? They weren't Soulpushers. They couldn't even read auras, as far as she knew.

The Duval County line. Fifteen minutes or so and she'd be at the hospital. She hoped the hospital had good coffee.

———— • ———— • ————

The parking lot was packed. Jack and Zoe parked near the edge, near the office complex next door to the hospital. Navigating through rows and rows of parked cars took them 10 minutes. They almost didn't make it, getting nearly rammed by a red sports car aiming for a front space that had just opened up.

Zoe turned toward the sound of air rushing past and started to make a gesture she'd seen on TV. Jack lightly pulled her arm down, but he glared at the car as it pulled into its prized space.

"I'm mad too, but a confrontation with an entitled jerk won't help today. Let's get inside so that we can talk to Mercedes."

Once again he was saying names that had nothing to do with the person they were going to see. She mentally shrugged. Maybe Mercedes was a fellow investigator.

Zoe got nervous as the elevator went up. A body without a soul. Would she be able to figure out where the soul was?

The door opened. She stepped out onto the floor she'd visited before. Adora's room was on the right, near the nurse's station. She peered in, but the older woman wasn't there. Probably for the best...she'd probably get over-excited. She made a mental note to call Luisa.

Everything felt slow motion to her. She supposed that was a nervous reaction. She'd felt something like it with David before. The less you want to go somewhere, the longer it seems to get there. Her hands were numb, and her legs felt prickly. Like she'd sat too long on the floor. Her stomach felt like pancakes being tossed too high above the pan. She waited for the pancake to hit the flame...in other words, she thought she was going to vomit.

The young man's room was at the very end. The hallway seemed so narrow...much narrower than it should have been. Her eyesight was good, despite never having been used until 6 months prior. The door to his room opened and Zoe was surprised to see a made bed inside, instead of the person she'd expected to see. Where was he? Had they waited too late? Had the body died? If so, would she still be able to find the soul?

She was disconcerted to feel Jack break away from her. He veered toward a room on the left. She stopped. He put his hand lightly on hers and pulled.

"Where are you going?" he asked. "David's in here."

Zoe froze for a few seconds, her mind grasping for sense. Her mouth opened and closed, trying to find words. She couldn't find any words to put to her thoughts. She couldn't find any thoughts.

Zoe numbly followed Jack into the small room on the left. She was overwhelmed with all of the familiar, yet out-of-place sights. It was a "who's who" of David's life. His best friend Herb, his best friend's sister Renna— AKA the Love of His Life—Yvonne, the red-haired girl she'd saved, the prankster Dempsey, Mrs. Byres and a nurse who really seemed like a Soulpusher.

What was this? Zoe had never fainted before, but she felt like it was happening. She looked around at the scared, grief-stricken faces. Why were they all here?

Then she looked down at the bed. She felt the blood drain from her face. She felt her body start to go.

Lying there—not moving, not dead, but not fully alive—was her best friend. Her brother. The only person she'd known for 16 years.

David's soul was gone. His body was there, but he wasn't. She started to feel sick. She felt her lunch pushing its way up her esophagus. She couldn't tell if she was going to vomit or pass out...or both.

Instead, her brain went into overdrive. It scurried to grasp for an explanation...trying to make sense of what her eyes conveyed. The only explanation came at her in a rush.

She was responsible for this.

A feeling like a gut punch overwhelmed her...guilt flooded her system. Her body shut down while her brain, unable to latch on to the truth, screamed in despair. Her soul, not knowing what to do, reached out for the only safe place it knew...David. Zoe's soul, the hapless player in the Council's game, unlocked from Zoe's body and plunged back into its home of 16 years.

Zoe snapped open her eyes. She looked around. Complete darkness. She knew exactly where she was, though.

———— • ———— • ————

Jack bent down to lift Zoe's head. She was unresponsive. Parshall, after checking Zoe's pulse, yelled for a doctor. Mercedes slumped further into her chair. The kids didn't know what to do, so they stayed put.

More medical personnel came in, pushing a gurney. As they were lifting Zoe up, another figure appeared behind them. This person was not a nurse, unless leopard-print pant suits had replaced scrubs.

Renna and Herb lit up. "You made it!"

Regina walked around the gurney toward her grandkids. She looked down at David, and over at Zoe being wheeled out of the room. "What the..."

The intercom blasted through, overriding Mrs. Sheardon's next word.

"...are you mixed up in?" she finished.

———— • ———— • ————

The Sheardons could hear the others arguing out in the hallway. The nurse was mad at Nisha's uncle because apparently he didn't know anything about the girl who had just collapsed. He didn't know who her parents were or how to contact her family.

Renna looked at her grandma. Hair just as long as Renna's, though finer. Her skin was a lot redder because of all the time she spent in her convertible. She didn't look sixty-five. She could have passed for forty-five—though she was out-of-breath, so maybe fifty at that moment.

She looked at her two grandchildren, taking a moment to notice how grown-up they looked. She smiled. Then she grimaced.

"I knew there was something about that David boy. He didn't seem like a pusher himself, but I felt something there. Another soul. What happened?"

Renna, tears in her eyes, looked over at David's still figure. "That's the thing. We don't know. He just didn't wake up one day."

Their grandmother sat down in one of the abandoned chairs. She gathered her thoughts for a minute and then looked back up at Renna. "You really love this boy, don't you?"

Renna nodded.

"He's my best friend," Herb said, nodding also.

Mrs. Sheardon looked around. Her eyes fixated on the space next to Renna, opposite of Herb. "He's there," she said. "He's separated from his body, and he doesn't know how to get back in."

Her eyes drifted over toward the body. "But he's not empty. There's another soul trapped deep inside. She can't surface."

———— • ———— • ————

Yvonne had a headache. The bright lights were piercing through her eyes. The myriad of agitated voices reminded her too much of that day on the lake. All those people yelling at her, but no one being able to help her. She imagined that must be how the girl on the gurney felt...if she was conscious.

She turned her head away from the voices, away from the overhead lights. She looked down the hallway toward the nurse's station. She saw an elderly lady hobbling toward them, occasionally lurching at the wall, steadying herself on the beam that led along the side.

Yvonne slid down the wall until her butt hit the floor. She didn't even feel it. Dempsey tried to help her up, but she waved him away.

The woman reached them.

"You, young lady and young man, you come to my room and tell me what happened."

Dempsey raised an eyebrow.

Adora huffed, exasperated. "Nothing weird. I know Zoe and I want to find out what happened."

She tried to help Yvonne up. It wasn't working out too well.

"You two, come lie down. I don't have a roommate. Come tell me what happened."

Dempsey went to fetch a wheelchair for Yvonne, because she was too weak to stand. He turned back toward the older lady. She indicated that she would need one, too.

Great, Dempsey thought. *We're supposed to be helping one person. Now we've got another down, and we seem to have adopted an elderly Spanish lady.*

———— • — • ————

Mercedes leaned against the wall, outside of David's room. Parshall and Jack were still in the middle of the hallway, arguing. Mercedes heard a lot of questions, but Jack didn't have any answers.

She heard Regina groaning and breathing heavily. Mercedes stretched her neck a little so that she could peek in the room, without them seeing.

The three of them hovered around David. Mrs. Sheardon was pulling at the air around his chest, like she was plucking invisible flowers.

The groans gave way to words. "Ooh...it's in there good. It's in there deep. Renna, brace yourself against David. You, too, Andrew."

What was she doing—pulling a tooth? Mercedes shook her head. She had no idea where the staff had taken the girl. She got up to see if she could find out.

———— • — • ————

Renna didn't know how much more groaning she could take. Her grandmother was probably terrorizing whoever was in David's body.

She felt ridiculous even thinking that statement. Maybe talking out loud would help ground her. She gestured to her brother to sit down with her.

"I heard a rumor that you weren't going to college."

Herb arched his eyebrows. "I'm rumor-worthy now? Maybe I'm already a star."

She frowned. "Seriously. Why wouldn't you go to college?"

"Because I can get an education from the masters on the ground. You know, the musicians playing on street corners, and in clubs."

Renna didn't say what she was really thinking. Did he want to play on street corners? Wouldn't he rather play a big venue? She didn't say it, though, because it would be pointless. He'd say that the best music could be found in the dirtiest, smallest locations. And he'd be right.

There was also no point in mentioning that she'd planned her career around his. Did street musicians even need managers?

He picked up on her thoughts. "You can still manage me someday, if you want. You've been managing me my whole life anyway. But you need to go to college. You need to learn the business."

She shrugged. "Maybe I'll be so successful that I won't want to work for you. I'll have even more obnoxious clients."

He punched her lightly on the shoulder. "That's the spirit."

The noises got louder. Renna looked up, toward her grandmother. "Grandma, why don't you try putting David back in? Then maybe the girl will be able to get out. At least she wouldn't be alone in there."

A pen fell off the hospital table in agreement.

Grandma Sheardon grunted. "Alright, alright. Worth trying."

—— • —— • ——

Adora stood at the door to her room, peeking out down the hallway. The two kids sat on the bed nearest the door. Neither one wanted to be in that tiny room, but neither wanted to be out in that mess. Parshall was still yelling.

Adora ducked down behind the door quickly. The kids rushed to her.

"Are you OK?" Yvonne asked.

"The mother ran by. I didn't want her to catch me snooping again."

Dempsey laughed, and Yvonne swatted his arm.

The old lady held up her hand and the kids helped her up, onto the bed.

"You children tell me what happened. Where's Zoe? Who's the crazy lady in animal print? Why is the nurse screeching like that?"

They looked at each other. Dempsey took the lead for a change, but realized he didn't know what to say. "We don't know. We came here with the nurse to tell Mercedes..."

He stopped, realizing he was about to spill secrets.

"Oh, relax, little pale child. I know all about your 'secret society.' Spirit is older than any society, no matter how much influence it thinks it has."

Yvonne blanched. "It's not *our* secret society! We had to break in to find out anything about it."

"Interesting...I like this even more. What *did* you find out?"

They hesitated.

"Look," Adora continued, "I know all about Soulpushing. Zoe filled me in. But she was interested in the other kid...the one who left a few days ago. What did that have to do with the Byres kid?"

"You know David?" Yvonne asked.

"Yeah, he and his mother used to come into the store whenever their island kin came up."

"What are you talking about—other kid?" Dempsey asked.

"There was another boy here. That's who Zoe was looking into. He didn't have a soul. Well, it wasn't on him, anyway."

"Do you know where he is now?" Dempsey asked.

Adora nodded. "Sure. Everyone knows where he lives."

They heard a noise and looked up. The Sheardon twins were in the doorway, staring at them defiantly.

They really aren't as easy-going as David made them seem, Yvonne thought. In fact, she was getting a flashback to the twins in *The Shining.* She was waiting for the river of blood to come down the hallway.

"We're tired of being left behind. We're coming with you," Renna demanded.

"Alright, alright. Don't get your microphone twisted around your waist." Dempsey started.

Herb glared at Dempsey. "My microphone is cordless."

———— • ———— • ————

Mercedes made it down to the lobby, outside of the ER. She was tired. She was bedraggled, too. She caught her reflection in a glass window and realized she looked more like a patient than a visitor. She leaned back against a wall. She could hear voices in the hallway on the other side.

"We put her into Emergency. Don't know what's wrong. Her vitals are good. She's breathing. She has brain function. She just won't wake up."

"Still no idea who she is?"

"None. All we got is the name Zoe. We'll keep her down here for a few hours, then we'll probably put her up in extended care."

Mercedes slumped against the wall. What was she doing down there? She couldn't help that girl. That girl couldn't help her son.

She dragged herself out an exit onto a patio area with a nice pond. She sat on a bench, staring at the turtles for a little while, wishing she could swim happily in safety and contentment.

She felt something brush up against her arm. She looked over to her right, but there wasn't anything there. She felt something in her hand. She looked down, and once again there was nothing there. She fell into sleep.

———— • ———— • ————

Parshall glared at Jack. She wasn't screaming anymore. Jack couldn't figure out what she was planning to do next, besides throw him out of the window. Instead, she pushed him into David's room and gestured for him to sit down. She closed the door.

"We think that someone pushed a soul into this boy's body when he was born. He probably knew there was someone there, but never told anyone."

Jack thought for a second. "Mercedes always said she had a hard time reading him. She always felt bad because she thought she didn't know her son. She didn't understand why some days he liked science and some days he liked music."

Parshall nodded emphatically. "There you go. I'm not experienced when it comes to double souls, but I guess that'd be one way it'd go. The souls would vie for dominance."

"You think that Zoe was that other soul?"

She shrugged. "Dunno. We found records for a girl named Annalisa, but no mention of anyone named Zoe. And since your brilliant mind didn't get any information on Zoe, we have no way to dig into that further."

"Well, wait. You said you had information on Annalisa, right?"

"Yeah. She was born here the same day as David. The file says she died the same day, though."

"Did the file give an address?"

Parshall narrowed her eyes. "OK, you were an idiot before, but that's a dang good idea."

"Dang?"

"You're lucky I don't cuss in the hospital. Otherwise you would have gotten an earful of impolite language."

———— • ———— • ————

Adora made sure she got all four phone numbers from the group. "Now don't you all text me. I'm not on an unlimited plan. Just one text if the group is in trouble. Don't be like my grandchildren...ten different texts to say one paragraph. You don't have to use one text to say 'Hi.' You don't have to say 'Hi' at all. I know who you are."

The kids scrambled out of there. That room was too tiny for them and Adora's personality.

They planned to go to that first boy's house—the boy who had been released. He lived in one of the old Arlington mansions.

"We don't want to be waiting around for a ride or a bus. Do we have enough money to rent a car?" Dempsey asked.

Yvonne shook her head. "You have to be twenty-five to rent a car."

Renna looked over at Herb.

"What?" he asked.

"Mom lets you borrow the car sometimes."

"Yeah, to go to the grocery store...when she wants something."

"Say you're going to the grocery store."

"You want me to lie?" Herb asked, shocked.

"Okay, well I don't *want* you to lie. I hate lying. But I want us to get to that house, and this is the best way I can think to."

Herb sighed. "I heard mom say we're out of butter."

Renna smiled.

———— • ———— • ————

Jack and Parshall had a plan involving the Zearotts, but both felt uneasy about implementing it. Going to a stranger's house and fishing for information about her daughter? Yeah, creepy.

Jack also knew that if he left without making sure Mercedes was safe, he wouldn't have a girlfriend anymore, no matter how much he was able to help David.

"We have to find Mercedes, first. She's grieving so much... I don't think she's in command of herself."

They heard a shuffling behind them. They turned to see an older Hispanic lady impatiently pushing at her walker, trying to go way faster than it was meant to. She needed roller wheels.

"I'll...." she puffed, stopping to rest. "I'll...find her."

Parshall looked skeptical. "We don't know where she is. Will you be able to search high and low on all of the floors?"

Adora frowned. "I've got friends. I can outsource. I'll find Mrs. Byres."

"Do you know her?" Jack asked. He'd only been dating Mercedes a few months, but he didn't remember her mentioning a loud, determined, cranky older woman.

She huffed. "My sister was a valued part of every family gathering Mercedes had. Now, time is getting away from you. Go to this Annalisa's house and find out if that's Zoe. I would like to have her back, too. I need to know if I'm going to live until the next lottery."

Jack was on the fence. He didn't know this woman. Then again, Mercedes was an adult. She'd been doing fine by herself this whole time. *If this goes wrong, we'll both be by ourselves,* he thought.

He reluctantly nodded. Adora was already on a video call with Luisa. She held up the phone. "Yes, these are the two. They're going to find Zoe's family."

Parshall and Jack half-smiled and half-winced at the tiny screen. A feistier version of Adora stared back at them, wearing curlers and a pink house coat.

Adora continued shouting at the phone, even though it was still facing the two reluctant field detectives.

"Luisa, get down to the hospital. Bring some empanadas. I know you don't have empanadas lying around. Go to the store!"

Yvonne and Dempsey waited at a coffee shop across the street from the hospital. Renna and Herb had taken the bus back to their house, with the hopes of returning in a car.

Yvonne reached across the table and put Dempsey's hand in hers. "Thank you for helping. I'm very proud of you. You've taken on a lot of responsibility, and you're doing a wonderful job."

He smiled. "You're welcome, but you don't need to thank me. This is important. She saved our lives. My idiocy is what almost got us killed. I have a lot to make up for."

"You don't have to make up for anything. All you have to do is keep being an awesome person."

"And not screw up anymore."

She shrugged her shoulders. "Eh...and that too, I guess."

She took a sip of her frozen drink. "I was thinking...I may write a book about this."

He raised his eyebrows. "You sure corporate SP would like that?"

"Probably not. When we're done, though, I don't want there to be a corporate SP."

The Zearott Residence

The Zearotts' street was quiet and deserted. The neighborhood kids were at school and the neighborhood adults were most likely at work. Jack wasn't sure if they'd find anyone at Zoe's house—she'd never mentioned whether her mother worked, or anything else about her home life. Jack was glad he hadn't been in charge of raising his niece. She'd probably be an elementary school dropout.

He and Parshall walked up the short steps to the front door. No doorbell, so Parshall knocked brusquely and turned around, looking up and down the street.

"I've lived here my whole life, but I don't know much about this neighborhood. I can't tell you who here is or isn't an SP. That's another problem with compartmentalizing us. We don't know each other. Unless someone works at my hospital, has been a patient, or has visited a patient, I won't have any knowledge of their existence."

A curtain fluttered in the window next to the door. They both turned to it. Parshall held up her hospital credentials in the hopes that it might clue Mrs. Zearott into the urgency of their house call.

The mother opened the door. She looked haggard. She didn't even ask who they were, she just let them into the front room and gestured toward the couch. She looked like she'd been expecting someone to show up.

"I guess you know about Annalisa. She's been missing since yesterday, so I figured she got caught."

Parshall looked over at Jack, then back to Mrs. Zearott. "We're not Council police. We're trying to help Annalisa. We know she's not dead."

Mrs. Zearott glanced over to the opposite wall, to the pictures dotting the mantel above the fireplace. Pictures of the two older daughters. One in her police uniform.

Though the two amateur detectives were working with limited information, they both figured out quickly that those were her two other daughters.

"What does the other one do?" Jack asked.

"Pharmaceutical sales."

"Ah...makes sense," Parshall said. "She can travel to different hospitals and physician offices...a traveling Soulpusher." She waited a beat before she said the last part. "Flexible hours, too, so that she could take care of Annalisa."

Mrs. Zearott looked down. "It wasn't easy for them. They lost their sister, but they didn't lose the responsibility of having to care for her. They missed out on a lot—proms, concerts, dates. They had to stay home while I worked. Now they're older, and they work, too. We all three had to take turns with Annalisa."

"Had?" Jack prompted.

She shrugged. "Well, it sounds like you already figured it out. She woke up—out of the blue—about six months ago. She calls herself Zoe. We've been keeping her secret, so please don't go telling any of those Council people. They're the ones who wanted me to kill her in the first place."

"Mrs. Zearott," Parshall started, "when was the last time you saw Zoe?"

"Yesterday. She runs all over this town. She has it in her mind she's gonna clean up the Council. I shouldn't let her. I should make her stay home, but I don't want to restrict another child's freedom."

"Something happened. Zoe's alive, but I think her spirit is out of her body. Would you come to the hospital and help us?"

"Of course, but I'm not sure how much help I'll be. Remember, I just met her six months ago. That boy who got her spirit—David—he can probably help."

Jack grimaced. "Well, that's kinda what started this whole thing."

Parshall held up her hand, trying to indicate that she had an idea, but couldn't quite find the words for it yet.

"OK," she started. "We have someone at the hospital who is working on getting David's soul back into his body. Once he's back in there, he might can help Zoe get back to her own."

Parshall looked like she was settling on an idea. "How about this. We work on getting Zoe's body moved back here before the Council finds out who she is. Then, once we've got David back whole, we'll bring him here so that he can help us put her soul back."

Mrs. Zearott's eyes fluttered shut in exhaustion. "I don't care what you do, just get my daughter back here safely. Try to bring her soul as soon as you can. I'm going to rest for a minute."

Parshall was able to lock the door from the inside, so she didn't have to wake up Mrs. Zearott as they left.

"What do you think?" Jack asked, as they made their way down the porch.

"I think we need to figure out how we're gonna get Zoe out of there."

———— • —— • ————

They waited until they were miles away from Zoe's house before they turned their phones back on. They didn't want to leave any traces that they were at the Zearott house.

"So?" Parshall asked.

"So?" Jack parroted back.

"How are we going to spring her? She needs to be released to a family member."

"I have an idea."

———— • —— • ————

Parshall hadn't been on campus since she was a student herself. Not much had changed. All the buildings grouped together, huddled against the surrounding woods. If you liked to walk to your destination, you weren't going far.

The University of North Florida, like most state colleges, was very much a commuter college. This meant that most students drove to campus. This also meant that parking was sparse. Jack drove around a few minutes, looking for a place. While he did that, he also brought up something that had been bugging him.

"Zoe's mother said something about having to Soulpusher her daughter. What did she mean by that?"

Parshall's face wasn't sure what expression to settle on. It settled on sad. "That is a whole 'nother story. Do you mind if we save that for later?"

UNF

In the 6 months since David's situation began, Nisha had taken on more of a leadership role within the band. She'd moved full-time to Jacksonville and went from working part time at the University of Florida in Gainesville to full-time at the University of North Florida. She decided to take a break from classes until she'd saved some money.

She was helping students with the computer systems that day—restarting them (the computers, not the students) when they crashed, showing kids where the document writer was, and reminding them to hit "save" so that they didn't ask her later to testify to their professor that they did, in fact, complete their homework.

She needed a break. Five days a week of student stress hormones was too much. She escaped through a side door.

Unfortunately, her uncle was walking by just as she opened the door. He heard the squeaking and turned. She tried to back-track, but it was too late. He'd made her.

The woman with him looked nervous and started to back away.

"What...what do you want?" Nisha asked. He was always asking if he could use the library, and she was always telling him no.

"It's not what you think! I don't need a book! I need you to help me."

She sighed a deep, long sigh. "That sounds worse."

"Oh, it is!" he exclaimed brightly. "I need you to make an I.D. for someone and then get her out of the hospital, pretending to be her sister."

Nisha stared at him for a moment. Then she turned back into the library. Whining 18-year-olds were preferable to whatever Uncle Jack wanted from her.

Parshall saved the situation. "Please? It'll help David."

The magic words. Nisha came out of the building. "How does this relate to David?"

They both hesitated, not knowing how much they should tell Nisha.

It was Parshall's secret to tell, so she told her about Soulpushing.

"Wait...you're saying that this Zoe girl was at every band practice?"

"Well, she was always with him. I don't know how much she paid attention to what was going on," Jack said.

Nisha shook her head. "That is a weird story. The weirdest you've told me, and you claimed to have seen Bigfoot."

Jack tipped his head, acknowledging the truth of the statement. "So...you'll do it?"

"You are an awful influence, you know that? I left that skill back in high school, and I got rid of the equipment."

She thought for a moment. "I know who can do it, though. I'll give you the contact information. You get the card made yourself."

———— • ——— • ————

"What name should we put on the card?"

The trio had gone inside and Nisha had found an empty study room for them.

The three of them spent several agonizing seconds deeply, desperately trying to think of a girl's name.

"I don't know!" Jack shouted. "Candy? Mandy? You know our family has never been good at picking names."

"Mindy? Cindy?" Nisha helplessly offered. Nothing seemed punchy enough. They wanted something that Zoe might be able to live with for the rest of her life.

"How about Zoe?" Parshall interjected.

Parshall could almost see the tension slack off from their shoulders.

"Huh," Jack acquiesced. "That'll work nicely. Zoe Albone."

"She might need to be Zoe Albone for the rest of her life. Are you okay with her being an Albone forever?" Parshall asked.

"Well, let's introduce her to the family gradually. If what you're saying is true, she's already met us," Nisha answered.

The Sheckles House

An hour had passed and neither Sheardon had shown up. Yvonne and Dempsey were worried. Worry turned to dismay when they looked out the window and saw the largest SUV they'd ever seen.

The passenger door opened. They caught a few seconds of Renna yelling as she opened the door and tumbled out.

"Stupid SUV. It's not made for short people. Why didn't you ask for the regular car?"

"When are you gonna learn to drive? I won't be around much longer to drive you places."

Ooh, sore spot, Yvonne thought.

————— • ————— • —————

They parked outside of the Sheckles house, which had been remodeled since it was built more than a hundred years before. It still had that old antebellum look, with the wraparound porch and balconies, but the front steps had been replaced with a ramp and the paint job was new.

Renna suggested that she and her brother go in, instead of the other two, because it was her turn to do something interesting.

Yvonne raised her eyebrows. "Knock yourself out."

Her nerve wilted a little, like the flowers on the bushes circling the house wilted every winter. She gave the weakest knock she'd ever given in her 16 years. All the bravado she'd felt before dropped like crumbs off a blanket.

It took a few minutes for who they presumed to be the nurse to answer the door. She looked at them warily.

"If you aren't selling Thin Mint cookies, then please leave."

"No!" Renna answered. We're not here for cookies." She looked over at her brother.

"But we do like Thin Mints," he answered, unhelpfully.

139

"We know Zoe," Renna started, hoping that would be enough to get them in the door. She was correct. The woman grumbled a little, but let them in.

Ten minutes later, the kids were sitting in the living room eating cookies and drinking milk. Despite Herb's lactose intolerance, he went for it. He was going for a mind over matter thing.

"We're hoping that what we find out can help Brandon also," Renna said.

"Why isn't Zoe here?" The nurse asked. "She seemed really invested in this."

Renna looked nervously over to her brother, who was belching lightly under a mustache of chocolate. She handed him a napkin.

"Whatever happened to Brandon has happened to her. And also to our friend David."

The nurse gasped. "They're at it again?"

Renna stood up and reached over to the nurse. She put her hand on her shoulder. "I don't think so. We think this was an accident. We've been talking to a Soulpusher named Parshall. Do you know her?"

The woman nodded. "Well, I don't know her, but I know who she is. She works at the hospital."

"Yeah," Herb answered. "Also, we have another friend who is a paranormal investigator. He thinks that Zoe—"

Renna kicked him. The woman looked alarmed.

Renna apologized to both of them. "I'm sorry. We just don't know who we can trust with this information. Please don't take this the wrong way."

She nodded her head. "OK, please tell me what you feel comfortable telling me."

"Anyway," Renna continued. "We think that Zoe was a victim like Brandon. She was out long enough for you to meet her, but then it happened again. We're hoping that if we can solve your mystery, we can solve ours, too."

"I don't think it's much of a mystery. The Council wanted to hurt the Sheckles, and this was how they did it."

"But was it really the Council?" Renna asked. "I mean sure, they did the crime, but who ordered it? If we can figure out who did that, then maybe we can stop it happening again."

"I've been going over this in my head for twenty years. The boy didn't have any enemies. He was a baby. The Sheckles didn't have any enemies. They had money, but they were good people. They were kind people." She started to tear up a little bit.

Renna moved over to her couch to comfort her. Herb took that as his queue to get up and wander around. He went over to a front window and looked out at the car. Yvonne and Dempsey were looking down at something. Probably the newspaper printouts they'd gotten from the college library.

He looked down the street. A dark sedan was approaching. He couldn't see the driver because the windows were tinted. The car slowed down behind the SUV, long enough for the driver to take down the plate number, if he wanted to.

He turned his attention back to the two talking. They were discussing any visitors at the hospital when Brandon was born.

"Family, mostly. I remember Marion saying one of our classmates from Englewood came by. I haven't given that a thought, though. We've known him our whole lives. I remember she said he'd seemed really upset."

"Do you remember his name?"

"Oh wow...what a question. He was more Marion's friend. I thought he was kind of a pushover. Let me go look for the yearbooks."

She came back a few minutes later with four books.

"We would have been in the same grade, so any one of these should suffice. Let's start with the senior yearbook, though. That would be the most recent one."

Though Englewood had been a small school back then, it still wasn't easy studying each picture. Especially since Renna had no idea what she was looking for.

The nurse was also reminiscing about each person, which didn't quicken the pace. Renna didn't intervene, though. Any memory could jog something about the visitor.

She pointed to a girl with wavy blond hair and a pretty smile. Her name, like Mrs. Sheckles', was Marion. Her last name was Jones.

"I remember she worked at the skating rink on the weekends. We used to go out there sometimes. I spent most of the time in the cafeteria because I'd busted my ankle trying to skate. I say 'trying' quite literally. I never got the hang of it. Kept falling on my butt. We all liked her, though, so we'd go visit her at the concession stand."

Her face brightened a little. "She was his sister! I remember now. They were twins. He wasn't into skating either, but he'd come to pick her up. He'd come in and hang out at our table. Marion—not his sister Marion, but Brandon's mother Marion—would usually come over and sit with him for a few minutes. Come to think of it, I think they had something going on. I don't know why it didn't pan out."

Renna was happy for the information, but she was also getting a little impatient. "That's great. Do you remember her brother's name?"

"Yes!" she exclaimed. "It was really similar to hers. It was Martin Jones!"

Great, Renna thought. *There can only be a hundred or so of those in Jacksonville, if he still lives in Jacksonville.*

"Oh my goodness! I can't believe I forgot this! I saw him a few years ago!"

"Where?" Renna asked.

The nurse blanked out for a second, not sure how to say what she needed to say. "I saw him on the road. I was driving by a really nasty accident, and he was inspecting the car. I remember now—Marion told me. He's an auto claims adjuster. He goes out after accidents and inspects the car."

"Do you know what company he works for?"

She shrugged. "I was just driving by. I didn't stop to ask the victim what auto insurance they use."

Renna didn't appreciate the haughty tone. They were trying to get as much information as they could out of this woman's hazy memory. The attitude wasn't helping.

Just then something struck a chord in Herb's memory. He rarely remembered anything beyond music and clothes, but he remembered this.

"Didn't Laura call the Englewood guy Martin?"

"Huh?" Renna asked, confused.

"The Englewood guy. When we were behind the restaurant, listening to their meeting."

"Oh? The Council?" Renna thought for a moment. "Yeah. You're right. She called him Martin. That makes sense. He's a Soulpusher, and he knew Mrs. Sheckles. That's the connection."

The nurse realized where this train was headed. "No! The guy I knew wouldn't do that. He was a sweetheart." Her tone dropped some of its confidence. "Right?"

Herb shrugged. "Maybe, or maybe someone else used his connection. We'll find out. In the meantime, someone just drove by slowly, like they were casing us or your house."

She didn't like that. "What? Who? Someone is casing our house?"

Herb shrugged again. "Don't know, but you and Brandon shouldn't stay here. Do you have anywhere you both can go?"

She rolled her eyes. "I guess. What are you two going to do?"

Renna looked toward the window. "Herb, will you stay here and help out? I'm going to ask Dempsey if he'll go with me to Mr. Jones' house. I need to figure out what's up with him."

"What's up with Mr. Jones?"

She swatted his shoulder in the way only a relation or close friend can do. "No. I want to find out if we can trust Dempsey."

Laura

Laura made a rare decision. It was rare because she hardly ever made decisions, but also rare because it went against every part of her body and soul. She decided not to go to the restaurant.

Her reasoning was sound. She was scared witless. She'd noticed a car parked near the bus stop the last few days, and the same car had also been parked near the restaurant.

So, she remained at Council headquarters, bored and drinkless. The TV had stopped working months before. The magazines were all old. The books were older, mustier and already read. She had the Internet, but anytime she went to look something up, she'd immediately forget what she had meant to look up.

So, she sat near the window and looked out to where she had seen the car. The side lot merged into the strip mall's parking lot next door.

The car was back again. The bus had come and gone, so whoever was in there must have figured out that she was staying in the office. Maybe they'd bring bagels.

The car door opened. The most imposing man she'd ever seen in her life got out. He did not have bagels.

She slid out of the chair and crouch-walked into the interior of the building. She hoped she'd locked all the doors. Somehow, she didn't think it would matter.

She usually liked being right, but not that time. She heard the side door rattling. She should have had that boarded up years before. Hindsight 20/20, and all that.

She felt in her pocket for her phone. *Dangit*, she thought. *It must have slid out of my pocket.* She really needed one of those holders that joggers wore that went around the arm. She'd seen joggers before, a few times. If she were still alive later, she'd look online. Though she'd probably forget as soon as she sat in front of the computer.

He'd busted the state-of-the art 1960's lock and was walking down the hallway, towards her location.

She backed away a little more, but she was up against a wall. Literally and figuratively. *Why wait*, she figured.

"What do you want?" she cried out, trying to keep her voice from breaking. Failing to keep her voice from breaking.

He appeared at the door to the main room, so tall he almost had to duck.

"I've been waiting a long time for my boss to get back around to you. They gave up on you people years ago, but I never did. I saw what you can do. I saw how you pulled that soul out of that baby's body."

"I don't—" She started to say she didn't understand, but he interrupted her.

"That was not what you put in your brochure, but I liked it. I could kinda see the soul go into that guy. The problem is, though, the soul's still around. What if he gets out? What if that guy turns on you and tells the truth?"

Laura was totally lost. She should have gone to the restaurant.

"The worst part was that no one believed me, even though they knew what you people could do. I was just a hired hand and my story was ridiculous. Man pulls soul from baby, deposits soul in self. It's ludicrous. After we left Jacksonville, the company buried the whole thing. I remembered, though."

"Why are you here now, if no one believed you?"

"Because that kid's name has been popping up on the radar. He recently went to the hospital, right?"

"Yes, but that was because he didn't have anywhere to stay."

"You're telling me with the resources that family has, he couldn't have gone into a private facility?"

She squirmed a little. "Well..."

"Well, nothing. That nurse could have rented a hotel room and stayed there with him. But instead, the Council arranged to have him brought into a public hospital known to have Soulpusher ties. The hospital made a special arrangement to hire the nurse temporarily."

"Well..."

"Well, I went by the Sheckles residence and I saw a bunch of kids outside and inside, talking to the nurse. It seems like our little secret is getting a lot less secretive."

"Well, crap. When you put it that way..."

"So, you're gonna work with me?"

His voice made it sound like a question, but his body language was making a very definitive statement. It said "You will do what I say."

She slumped a little, looking very sad, sprawled out on the floor of the old, nearly empty great room.

"Yes, I will work with you."

Zoe Albone

The discharge papers were being worked on. The Albones had been brought up to speed. They were surprisingly OK with quasi-adopting an unknown comatose teenager. Perhaps it was because she was already named, and didn't require any input from them on that front.

Mrs. Sheardon knew she'd have a better chance of getting Zoe's soul back into her body if it were close, so she only had a short window to get this thing done.

She leaned over David's body. "Zoe," she said, "I know you can hear me. You're probably a little scared and bewildered. You've never been in there by yourself. Your touchstones are gone. I want you to listen to me, though. He's out *here*. If you're very quiet, you'll be able to pick him up."

She waited for a few moments, hoping Zoe was able to follow her instructions.

"Do you remember how you were able to leave David's body before? I need you to do that now. You're not supposed to be there. You have your own body, and your own mother. Do you feel your body? It's right across the hallway."

She wished she could wheel the body into the room, but that would look even more suspicious. She decided to take a different tactic.

———•——•———

Zoe hadn't felt this frightened since she was a little baby ghost child and had "awoken" into a dark void. She was in the dark void again, but there weren't any voices for her to connect with. There weren't any images for her ghost eyes to interpret. There was nothing but the far off, somewhat familiar voice of an older woman. She knew that voice, but didn't know how.

She struggled to hear what the woman was saying. Something about helping her get out. Then she felt a presence so familiar that she jolted toward the surface. When she brushed what she guessed was a face, she saw the hint of light through the eyelids.

David. That's what she felt. She couldn't open David's eyes for him, though, and she couldn't move his body. Her only option was to hoist herself out. It wasn't like before when she had his energy to help her. She had nothing. Just her traumatized, confused soul.

She tried anyway. She pushed herself up as far as she could. Once again she saw the tinge of light. Heard the far-off voice. Felt David's familiar presence. She reached up to him, as best as someone with no body could.

He reached back, and she grabbed him, pushing him down further, all the while rising up to the surface. She didn't look back, for fear that she might get trapped again.

Her eyes snapped open...this time for real. She jumped out of where she had been lying and almost fell as she tried to land on feet that hadn't been used in days.

She got her balance and looked around. She was in a hospital hallway—the hallway she remembered from visiting the Shenkles boy. She looked behind her. She'd apparently been lying in a gurney. Why, she didn't know.

She looked into the room. A very astonished-looking older woman stared at her. Was that Renna and Herb's grandmother?

She crept into the room and looked at the bed. A very astonished-looking David stared back at her.

What the? she thought.

———— • —— • ————

Zoe's case had gotten the attention of the hospital's head doctor, a woman probably in her fifties, with glasses and straight blonde hair tied behind her head.

"I strongly advise that you let her remain here. Even though our tests didn't reveal anything negative, we still don't know why she's not waking up."

"Doc," Jack said, "You saw her file. She doesn't have the first bit of health insurance. We're already going to be working for years to pay off this bill."

"We won't expect the money tomorrow. You pay what you can each month."

"It'll still take us years."

She sighed. "I can't stop you. I just want you to understand that you're taking her against doctor's advice."

He tried not to waiver. This was a big responsibility he was taking on, but he couldn't let Zoe get found out by the Council.

"I understand that. We have a big family. There will always be someone to take care of her."

The doctor's cell phone rang. She turned away from Jack and Nisha.

"This is Dr. Brown. Uh huh..." She listened for a few moments. They couldn't see her face, but they saw her body relax.

"Really? That's great! I hate open cases, so this is great news."

She hung up and turned back to them. "It looks like this is a non-issue. She woke up."

Nisha gasped, and then smiled. Jack almost laughed out loud, but then put his hand on his mouth and muffled it.

"We'll still escort her out in a wheelchair. I'll make sure she's ready and brought down here."

Nisha and Jack sat down in one of the lobby chairs.

"Are you going to look for Mercedes?"

He shook his head. "At this point, we have to stay separate. The less attention we draw to David, the better. I have to trust the two sisters. Even Parshall needs to stay away."

"Well, that sucks," Nisha said.

"That it does," Jack confirmed.

David Wakes Up

David was extremely disoriented. He felt heavy; sluggish. He looked down at his hands. His memory was fuzzy, but he seemed to remember not having hands recently.

He looked up at Mrs. Sheardon. He hadn't seen her in a few years. She still liked very colorful clothing and jewelry. However, something seemed off about her. She seemed deflated from her usual boisterous personality.

He realized what it was. She was crying. Gold makeup pooled under her eyes, and her foundation was smeared from her wiping her face so much.

"Are you alright?" he asked.

She smiled. "I am now. How are you feeling?"

"I've got the biggest headache of my life."

Right then a bustling noise came into the doorway. Regina rushed out of the chair, and over to David. She pushed him back down into the bed and said "Shhh...pretend you're still in a coma."

"Huh?" he started to say, as she put her hand lightly over his mouth, shushing him more emphatically. "I'll tell you later."

The nursing assistant came in. "It's time for his sponge bath."

Mrs. Sheardon winced. "Can't it wait? I...want to read the paper to him."

She looked around for a newspaper. Not finding one, she grabbed her phone out of her purse. "It's here. The newspaper. It's in my phone. They can do that now."

The aide nodded curtly. "They can do a lot on phones. The news site will still be there after I'm done. He's not my only patient."

Regina slumped her shoulders. "Alright," she said, walking toward the door. She heard David whimper, and hoped the woman hadn't noticed.

———•———•———

Mrs. Sheardon slunk back into the room after the aide had left.

"What was that about?" David whispered harshly.

"I don't want them to know you're awake yet."

"Why?" he whispered even more sharply.

"Because Zoe's awake and she's being discharged now, as we speak. As far as we know the Council hasn't connected you to her. We want to keep it that way. She's adopting a new life and a new name. You don't need to ruin it."

He slumped down in the bed. "Where is she going?"

"You'll find out soon enough. You'll be able to see her again, but not until we're in the clear. I know this is frustrating...just please, keep up the ruse for a few more days."

He didn't say anything, which made her more nervous than the whisper-screaming.

"Hang tight, my friend. I'm going to help your friends find another trapped soul."

"Hang tight? Who have you been talking to, Mrs. Sheardon?"

Mr. Englewood

Martin Jones lived in a modest, older home, in a modest, older section of Jacksonville. He owned a knickknack store about a mile away. He didn't call them knickknacks, but everyone else did, and he'd given up the fight. Collectibles, knickknacks, whatever.

His house was full of the merchandise he sold. In fact, the living room was so packed that one vacuum misstep could cause a chain effect, sending his wall-to-wall shelving plummeting, along with the fragile ornaments.

He'd bought one of those little robot cleaners, and it was small enough to go under the shelves. Crisis solved.

The little flat vacuum was set to start every morning at 8 AM. Of course his subconscious didn't know what the whirring noise was, so for a few minutes he'd have dreams of a tiny motorcycle chasing him, or a child's plastic car roaring to life.

This morning he woke up before the vacuum because he heard a real car pulling up in the driveway. He hoped it wasn't an over-eager vendor, asking him to look at their glossy photos of angel cherubs or jewelry boxes.

He peeked through the blinds. The largest SUV he'd ever seen was parked behind his car. The motor was still powering down. The passenger's door opened, and a girl fell out. He couldn't see much of her through her tangle of hair. The driver's door opened, and a young man went around the vehicle to help her out.

"I hate that monstrosity," he heard the girl say. "I need a step ladder to get down from it."

"I didn't particularly like driving it either."

"Point taken. Thank you for volunteering. I couldn't ride with my brother another minute. He can play a musical instrument like nobody's business, but he cannot guide a steering wheel."

The voices were getting closer, so they must have been near the door. He waited on the other side for them to approach. He figured they were probably fundraising.

The girl froze when he opened the door, her arm still raised in a knocking position.

"May I help you?" he asked.

"Uh..." she croaked out, obviously not having thought that far in advance.

"Miss..." he led, hoping for at least a name.

"Wow...you sure are inquisitive," she answered, looking over his shoulder into the house. "Can we come in?"

He looked past her, to the other earnest, young face.

"If this is a robbery, I'm warning you. I have skills that you don't see in movies."

———— • ———— • ————

Dempsey had a hard time getting comfortable on the small floral-patterned sofa. Mr. Jones had undoubtedly picked the smallest furniture to allow more room for tchotchkes. His knees extended way beyond the edge of the couch and scraped up against the glass coffee-table.

Renna spoke first. "A close friend of ours has gotten involved in a fiasco of the sort you'd be familiar with."

"Involving figurines?" the man asked.

Renna looked him squarely in the face, like she'd seen in so many espionage movies. "This has nothing to do with your main business. It's your side business."

He looked shocked. "You mean..."

"The business you take care of when there's a car wreck outside the shopping center, or when one of the older residents around here passes on."

His face flushed, all color draining out. He picked up his cell phone and dialed.

"Hi, yeah, it's me. I won't be in for a few hours. You'll be alright without me? OK, thanks. Bye."

He put his phone back down.

"What kind of fiasco?"

"We're here about something that happened more than 20 years ago. The Sheckles boy. What happened, and where is he? I mean, where is his soul?"

"You don't beat around the bush." He sighed. "I don't talk about that. We did a lot of bad things back then. That may have been the worst."

"I know," Renna continued. "You stole the soul of a newborn baby. There must be a special place in hell for that."

Mr. Jones started to shake. He was silent for many minutes, seemingly figuring out what to say.

"What we did was horrible, but I tried to mitigate it. This was all that family's doing. The Altmeyers. Greedy, heartless people. I always wondered if they'd accidentally sucked their own souls out. I found out what they were planning to do, and I volunteered to go."

"We know all this," Renna interjected, angrily. "Where is he? Did you put him in another baby? In a nurse?"

The look on the man's face softened. His tone changed. "It's OK. I'm fine. He really was just trying to save me."

Renna stared at him, confused. She grasped for something to say, but nothing came. She looked over at Dempsey. He could recognize hidden meaning in a heartbeat. He was staring keenly at Mr. Martin Jones.

"You're Brandon, aren't you? You've been in there the whole time?"

Right then the little robot vacuum cleaner started up, startling everyone. Dempsey knocked his leg against the table, tipping it. The flower centerpiece started to slide down the face of the table, but he caught it.

In all the commotion, no one heard the garage door open. No one saw the hallway door open until he burst into the living room.

Grandma Sheardon

Regina Sheardon pulled up to the Sheckles' house. She was exhilarated because of her success with Zoe and David. She was confident she could do the same thing with this boy. She suspected his soul was probably just hanging out at the house, waiting for further direction.

She squinted at the porch. No soul there. Well, except she saw the haze of an earthbound spirit that had passed naturally. Probably the mother or father. She didn't want to mess up her concentration worrying about ghosts. She needed to be in the zone for this project. She went up the stairs to the front door and knocked.

A few minutes later a woman in her 50's answered the door. She looked tired...worn down. She'd seen it on many a caregiver's face.

"Are you here about Brandon, too?" she asked, looking around Mrs. Sheardon for other people.

"I guess you've been getting a lot of visitors lately, huh?"

"Yes. Please come in before you attract the wrong kind of attention."

Regina Sheardon frowned. *Well, you're welcome,* she thought, a little annoyed.

———— • —— • ————

The nurse led her down the hallway. She heard a familiar voice and an unfamiliar voice talking awkwardly in the living room.

She recognized her grandson's voice saying "You have red hair. I kind of have red hair."

"Yes," the other voice said, trailing off.

The girl looked happy for the interruption when Mrs. Sheardon came into the living room. The girl had the reddest hair and palest skin she'd ever seen, this side of the Emerald Isle.

Herb jumped up as if he'd been caught doing something wrong. Regina wondered what he thought he was doing, since it was obvious the girl was having none of it.

He looked puzzled. "Grandma?"

"Yes," his grandmother answered. "I am your grandmother. You win the trivia question of the day."

The Young Butterfly Has Emerged

David was trying not to move. It was so hard. Everything itched. His hands were going into spasms. He didn't want to think about what the catheter was doing.

He hadn't been that bored in his life. He strained to hear the hint of a T.V from another room. He attempted telekinesis, but his phone didn't budge. He hoped Mrs. Sheardon came back soon.

He heard the door open, and then soft breathing. He couldn't tell who was in his room. His instinct was to open his eyes, but he knew he couldn't. Maybe this was the mysterious danger that his friends' grandmother had warned him about. Maybe he'd die there, never getting to say goodbye to his mother.

The bed sank down under someone's light weight. Whoever it was, they put their hand on his right hand. Could they feel it shaking?

"We'll get you out of this mess," the voice said.

The woman was quiet for a minute. She leaned down toward his head. The hair on his body prickled. He saw her shadow between his eyelids and the light overhead.

"David?" the voice whispered. He remained quiet.

"I can't believe she did it."

She left before David's sweat became palpable enough for her to feel.

———— • ——— • ————

Parshall couldn't find Jack anywhere in the hospital, which made sense. He was trying to draw attention away from David and Mercedes. She needed to tell him what she sensed, though.

She didn't know where he lived, and he wasn't returning any of her calls. She didn't want to go to the Albones' in Gainesville, because she didn't want to start a trail to Zoe.

She settled for the next best thing.

The college was at full capacity that day. It was the final week before the end of term, and the kids were studying on overdrive. The candy wrappers in the seat cushions conveyed that some of the kids were at least eating.

She found Nisha in the computer lab, trying to wipe a resistant hard drive.

"This machine is infected. I had to take it offline."

Parshall smiled. "I have some disinfectant in the car, but I know that won't help."

Nisha grimaced. "Knowing this kid—yeah, we're going to need some disinfectant for the seat and the keyboard."

Parshall grimaced and started to back out of the room. "If you follow me, I'll get the spray."

— • — • —

Parshall felt better being out of such a public place. Talking in her car made more sense.

"Do you have a way of contacting your uncle?" Parshall asked Nisha.

"Sure. We have a signal."

Parshall narrowed her eyes, annoyed.

"No! I'm not being sarcastic. I'm being for real. We have a signal. Why? What do you need to tell him?"

"The butterfly has come out of its cocoon."

"Huh?" Nisha asked.

Parshall pursed her lips and tried again. "OK, one more time. The young male butterfly has awoken from his cocoon. However, he's not moving. I suspect there's a reason he's not letting anyone know."

"Brandon?" Nisha asked, still bewildered.

"Oh, crap," Parshall exclaimed, starting to get annoyed. "Not him. The other one."

"Oh," Nisha said, nodding. "I get it. You want Jack to know?"

"Yes, but I don't want him to let anyone else know. There's a reason David's still lying in the hospital bed, and I don't want to ruin the plan—whatever it is."

Nisha nodded. "I get it. I'll contact him. Uncle Jack's not going back to the hospital. I went there yesterday and told Mrs. Byres that we had a family emergency. It's not a lie, really. We just got a new family member."

"Did Jack go back to Gainesville?"

"No. He's still keeping his distance, even though anyone who does the first bit of investigation will figure out that he's tied to our family. He's taking care of some business for his paranormal group."

Parshall handed Nisha the disinfectant.

"If you want to wait here, I'll bring it back—"

"No," Parshall interjected, remembering the chair and the keyboard in the computer lab. "You keep it. My donation to higher education."

Nisha snorted. "Higher education, my butt. That kid was playing online games. I bet his mother wouldn't let him use the family computer for that, so he came here."

The Other Butterfly Emerges

Regina Sheardon was very uncomfortable with the way the nurse was staring at her.

"You mean you knew that those people were doing that?" the nurse asked, enraged.

The older woman shifted. "Well, we knew *something* bad was happening, but nobody here was talking about it. We did *not* know that they were keeping spirits Earthbound. We thought they were sending them back to the spirit world."

"So that would make it better? Uprooting a baby's soul, but making sure it got where it came from?"

Regina didn't say anything for a minute. "Look, I'm sorry. I really am. We were left out in the dark. We risked our lives just to get the information we had. We trolled the lowest of places to get information on that company. We blackmailed them until the company finally decided it wasn't worth the trouble. We may not have been able to save your friend's son, but we saved the city from being destroyed by those goons."

Yvonne spoke up. "Is that why the company left?"

"We think so. They got what they originally came for." She winced at how that sounded. She glanced quickly over to the nurse. "I apologize. That sounded horrible. I didn't mean to imply that Brandon was their objective."

She scowled. "But he was. Destroying the family was their objective, and they met it."

Regina nodded solemnly. "They went back to their home state, and the Soulpushers there have kept them in check ever since."

"So what's up with the person following us?" Herb asked.

She shrugged. "I remember him from back then. He's a low-level player...muscle, really. They don't consider him the brains. He took it

162

very badly when the company left. He was embarrassed, more than anything."

She lowered her head and her voice before she continued. "Some of us spies may have taken it upon ourselves to get information in more personal ways."

Herb gasped. "Grandma!"

"I may have led him on a little, but we got what we wanted. If the company had found out he was wining and dining me on their dime, he would have been the next victim. So we had him."

"And now he's back," Herb finished.

"And now he's back," his grandmother continued. "I don't know why, unless he wants to finish what the company started. Maybe he thinks they'll give him a promotion."

Herb was stumped. For one of the first times in his life, he didn't know what to say. Yvonne, not knowing what to say either, waited for the older woman to speak again.

"I need to find this boy's soul. That's why I'm here." She turned toward the nurse. "If it's OK with you, I'm going to search the property for what rightfully belongs to him."

The nurse nodded. "Do what ya gotta do. I'm going to be packing some bags for us."

———— • ———— • ————

It took about an hour for Regina to "sense" around the perimeter and inside the structure. She sighed heavily as she pushed her grandson's legs off the couch and sat down.

"Glad you can sleep," she told him.

"I can always sleep, Grandma."

"Come on, buddy. We gotta help them get out of here."

"Then what are you going to do?"

"I'm going to that man's house...that man the nurse knows. He's gotta know where the soul is."

"What are we going to do?"

Yvonne opened her eyes, in case she needed to chime in with an opinion.

"You two are minors, which means you need to go home."

"Hey," both kids yelled, getting off the couches.

"Hey, nothing. Herb, your parents would kill me if anything happened to you."

"I'm 18," Yvonne said.

"I'm 58. So?" Mrs. Sheardon answered.

———— • ———— • ————

Mercedes was getting used to weird, so when a dozen roses showed up at her door with the message "RSR Noon" written on the tag, she just shrugged. She suspected they were from Jack and it didn't take her long to figure out that RSR meant "roller skating rink." She'd recently told him how much David had liked that place when he was younger.

Jack went to all this trouble to be covert. Was Mercedes supposed to be covert in getting to the roller rink? Should she take three taxis? A bus and an Uber? Walk half the way and then fly? She didn't know.

She settled for driving downtown. She got out on foot and got lost in a mix of office workers walking to food trucks and football fans waiting for a trolley back to the stadium.

She spotted a taxi and waved it down. Taxis don't take names and still accept cash.

She'd never actually been in the skating rink. She'd dropped David off a few times, but other than that, he'd been a free-range kid during those hours.

She was not prepared for how dark it was, or how heavily the bass music thumped. It was a wonder David could hear anything after he came home on those Saturday afternoons.

She squinted at the figures sitting on the rounded benches, looking for a Jack-shaped person. She found him back in a corner, the farthest seat-pod from the rink.

Trying not to draw attention to her adult-sized frame, she slunk along the wall toward her previously MIA boyfriend.

"What are we doing here?" she hissed, as she slid in beside him.

He leaned in, so that he could speak as low as possible, while still being heard by Mercedes. "I didn't want to tell you any of this over the phone, or where we might be seen. I didn't want to tell you any of this at all, because I didn't want you to be dragged into my world."

Mercedes looked skeptical. "What world? Are you a kingpin? A spy?"

Jack bristled a bit at that. "No," he said. "I am not a kingpin. Not even a linchpin. I'm a paranormal investigator."

"Yes," she said slowly, drawing out the word to show how pointless his statement was. "I know this. You told me when we first met."

"Yeah," he continued, "but I didn't want you to experience first-hand what I do."

She paused, not sure of where to go next in the conversation. "So, you investigate the paranormal in a skating rink?" she asked, knowing that the rink had nothing to do with the situation, but also wanting to needle him a bit.

The shadows relayed that he was shaking his head. "There is activity here of the non-human kind, but that's not why I asked you here. I asked you to come here because it's dark. We look like any two people here. No one knows it's us."

"Well, except the ticket seller," she interjected.

"Hmpf," Jack scoffed, indicating that he had written off that danger. "He's a friend."

Mercedes cocked her head. "You are a skating rink kingpin, aren't you!"

He sighed. "I can't tell if you're serious or mocking me."

"I can't tell, either," she answered, frustrated. "Would you please start over, from the beginning?" she asked.

———— • ———— • ————

Zoe was trying to sleep in the guest room. She was having a hard time. No city noise. No headlights roaming across the wall.

After a few minutes, she got out of bed and wandered into the kitchen. She wasn't sure if she was family enough to just raid the fridge. Instead, she opted for some water, which came from a spigot built into the refrigerator. *Fancy*, she thought.

She caught light glinting through the glass nestled in the carved wooden patio doors. She moved past the dining table and pushed down on the latch. Were the patio doors monitored by the alarm system? She'd find out.

She pushed out into the stillness of the country night. More stars than she'd ever seen. Gentle lapping from the lake.

She shut the door behind her, careful not to lock herself out. She felt her way towards a rocking chair and collapsed into it.

She wasn't sure how she felt about being there. What was she going to do for the rest of her life? Would she be able to get a job with the credentials they'd cooked up for her? Go to college? No Johns Hopkins for her, probably. She had no past, which made her think she had no future.

She looked out at the lake. She remembered Yvonne almost dying out there. She remembered separating from David.

She hoped David was OK. Nisha had come back with the good news that he was awake.

Zoe sighed at the beauty of the starlight touching the rippling water...or was that the back of a gator...

The Albones had a see-through fence around their property to keep predators on the other side. This did not stop Zoe from being nervous. So, she decided to finish her emotional crisis inside.

The two kids helped the nurse get Brandon ready and into the wheelchair.

"Where are you going?" Herb asked.

"My sister booked a room for us at a small hotel. Her name is completely different from mine, so hopefully she won't draw their attention. What about you two? What are you going to do now?"

Herb started to answer the question, but Yvonne put her hand on his mouth. This did not go unnoticed by the nurse.

"Herb's grandmother said we can go with her."

Herb started to protest.

"Isn't that dangerous?" The nurse asked, absentmindedly. She was trying to get socks on the young man's feet.

Yvonne spoke up again. "Yes, but I'm an adult."

The nurse raised her eyebrows and then nodded over to Herb.

"He's not an adult."

"Who are we to argue with Regina?" Yvonne said, quickly, hoping the subject would drop like the young man's shoes.

The nurse shrugged. "Whatever. Glad y'all ain't my kids."

"What do you mean he's awake, and what do you mean he can't let anyone know?" Mercedes hissed, not caring that the kid skating backwards beside her might hear.

"I'm involved in this because of my paranormal research."

"Is that why you're dating me? To get closer to him?"

Jack realized he walked right into that. "No! This happened after we started seeing each other. However, I got involved because I care about you and David. Right now he's not on those people's radars and we really want to keep it that way. I'm going to stay away for a bit longer. I wanted to tell you, though, so you'd know to leave a radio on for him, or something."

"I'm not supposed to talk to him?"

"We never know who's listening. It would be better for you not to."

"You're telling me that my own son has awoken from a mysterious coma, but he's not allowed to show it, and I'm not allowed to acknowledge it?"

"Yeah," Jack answered, squeezing her hand.

"Won't the nurses and doctors be able to tell that he's not in a coma anymore?" Mercedes asked, not sure what the telltale differences were between sleeping and being comatose.

Jack slowed his roll, slowing Mercedes down with him. His face, what Mercedes could see of it under the disco lights, cramped up, like he'd been punched in an unfortunate place.

"No....? Maybe...? Yeah...?" he answered, weakly.

Mercedes stared at him as he grasped for an answer that made his plan seem workable.

He realized it wouldn't work. The first person to shine a flashlight in David's eyes would know that he was conscious. "OK new plan. You go to the hospital and let him know he can 'wake' up. I'm still gonna stay away for the next week or so. I'll let Nisha know if anything changes, and she'll get in touch with you."

———— • ———— • ————

"Thank you for letting me know. Yup, you're right. I would have never said they could come with me. OK, I'll be on the lookout. Yup, bye."

Regina pressed "end" on the dashboard phone interface. *Those stupid kids*, she thought. She didn't even know Yvonne's family. If anything happened to her, how could she possibly stand in front of her parents and tell them what happened? What would she say to her own son and his wife? Your son was trying to be a hero, and he got killed by a large, corporate goon? Yeah, that would go over well.

She found a little area to park in, near a small creek, about a block down from Mr. Jones' house. She scooted her little car in there and began walking down the sidewalk. A car with a rideshare sign passed her and turned onto a different street. She recognized the girl's hair.

Those little idiots, she thought. Yvonne and Herb were going to get there before she could make it. She did give them points for having the driver drop them off on a different street, though.

She sped up as best she could. She wasn't a runner by any means. She was barely a walker. There was a reason she had a car.

She scuttled, but she was only halfway to the house by the time the two kids arrived. She tried to put a little extra in her step, but her step was limited by the shape she was in. She made a mental note to try using the gym at her apartment complex, if she could find it.

She squinted. She saw a familiar tank of a car in the driveway. Really? She didn't just have to worry about one grandchild and one unknown child? Now she had two grandchildren and two unknown children? This was just getting worse.

She really didn't want to do this, but she couldn't think of another way to stop them. She pushed her hand out and pulled with her mind. She felt the familiar zing of two souls pulling toward her. She stopped before the souls had a chance to actually go anywhere.

She squinted again. The two young people had collapsed near the garbage cans. Adrenaline carried her the rest of the way.

As she got closer, she saw the shimmer of people-shaped light indicating that her crazy plan had succeeded. They were safe...sort of. Well, their souls were safe. She hurriedly pulled some trash bags around their bodies before any passersby who cared saw. The two kids were hovering behind her the whole time.

"What," she turned around, yelling louder than she should have. "You jackasses left me no choice. I couldn't have you go in there. It's probably going to be a crime scene in a minute."

The two figures retreated into the bush.

Regina waited a few moments to regain her composure. She decided to sneak around the side to find a window she could look through. She found a crack in a pretty white curtain that allowed her to see into the living room.

She had to brace herself to keep her legs from buckling. The man had a knife to the homeowner's neck. Regina looked around for her granddaughter. Renna's poor face was paler than anyone in their family's had ever been. She wasn't crying or screaming, though. Regina was proud.

She looked over at the boy. He looked scared, but he was composed. Regina didn't know him, but she could tell he was strong.

She tried to listen to what was going on. It was muffled.

"What do you want?" Mr. Jones asked, his voice frail from fear.

"What do you think I want, you idiot? I want the company to know what you're capable of, and I want to control it. Also," he continued, gesturing to the ceiling, "I want that boy's soul to go where it belongs."

"That's a lot for one morning. How about we start with sending the boy's soul where it belongs."

Regina sighed some relief out of her body. He was going to do what he should have done years ago—give the spirit back to the body. She wasn't sure he'd be able to do it under duress, though.

She made her way over to the back door. She took her all-in-one knife out of her boot and found a good one to jimmy the lock with.

She entered as quietly as she could and made her way through the kitchen, into the living room, behind the giant of a man.

"Dougie..." she said, softly.

The man's shoulders stiffened. "Reggie?"

He turned around so that he could see her. His eyes softened as he saw her, but hardened almost immediately as he remembered her betrayal.

Regina sensed this change immediately and reached out to touch his shoulder. "Dougie, that was a long time ago. It was complicated. I'm a Soulpusher. You worked for the company trying to destroy us. Don't take your revenge out on these people. Let's go somewhere and talk."

She got close, hoping her proximity was intoxicating enough to get him to drop the knife. Instead, he tightened it and Mr. Jones yelped.

"I'm not falling for that again. I've watched enough espionage movies since then to know you're playing me."

She shrugged. She'd tried the nice way. Oh, and it would have been nice...for him, anyway.

So, Dougie would be getting the less preferred option.

Regina had a special power that she'd cultivated through practice and by just being really good at what she did. Not only could she push spirits out of bodies, but she could also push spirits while they were in bodies, thereby pushing the bodies also. She pushed his soul so forcefully that his body landed on the couch.

Regina hurried up to Mr. Jones. She could sense Brandon in there, alright.

She put her hand up in front of his chest and pulled. Mr. Jones gasped as the gray essence rose out of him. Regina gently let her hand lower, and the gray mist settled beside her.

She looked over to the door. The spirits of the two kids had wandered in, sensing the shift. They stared at her, and then at the dissipating figure beside her. Regina looked back over at Dougie and realized that he'd taken his phone out and snapped a picture.

"Oh, you've got to be kidding me," she moaned. She went over to the man and thrust her fist into his chest. His eyes widened.

"Yeah, that's right. I can do this. Lucky for you I know how to dematerialize my hand. Feel that?"

The man whimpered.

"Yeah. That's your soul. I have it in my hand. Now, I'm going to let go, and I want you to leave this city...leave this state...and never come back."

He nodded fervently, shaking as he clutched his chest.

Renna and Dempsey backed away, into the kitchen, scared almost out of their minds.

Regina pulled her hand out and came into the kitchen to wash it. Some of the man's blood had materialized with her skin. Renna and Dempsey ran farther back into the hallway.

They stopped when they heard a noise from the living room. They went back in.

Laura, of all people, stood in the doorway, hair frazzled and face wild with energy. She turned toward the man.

"You are not going to own me. You are done in this town, and I'm done taking orders from you."

She stomped over to him and grabbed his phone. She threw it down and stomped on it with her heel, shattering the glass and cracking the phone into two pieces. The memory card had popped out. She tried to grind it with her heel, but only succeeded in skidding it across the carpet.

Dempsey ran over and picked it up off the floor. He grabbed the knife from where the man had dropped it and began chipping at the card, trying to break it apart.

That thing was a tough nugget, so he went into the kitchen and dropped it down the sink. He turned on the garbage disposal.

Once the grinding had stopped, everyone was quiet for a minute.

———— • ———— • ————

Herb and Yvonne looked at each other. To them, they looked substantial, as did Brandon, standing over by Herb's grandmother.

Everyone else seemed out of place, faint...like they were in an old faded photograph.

They were aware enough to know, though, that Regina had saved all of their lives.

Yvonne's spiritual head started to get a spiritual headache. Apparently that was a thing. She went over to Brandon and hugged him. "I know someone who's going to be very happy to meet you," she told him.

Regina went over to the couch and sat beside Dougie.

"Why did you do all this?" Regina asked the man.

"I had to prove to the company that I was right, and that you were still a threat. Also I was hoping for a promotion."

She sighed. "I started this when I manipulated you all those years ago. I'm sorry for that, but I was trying to protect my people."

He nodded. "Now that I'm not a threat anymore, may I leave?"

Laura stepped in. "Not before you promise to never step foot in this city again. You leave me and the Council alone."

Regina interjected. "You leave us all alone. That includes the Sheckles and the Zearotts."

Laura looked sharply over at her. "What would the Zearotts have to do with this?"

Regina scowled. "This goes for you, too, Laura. You leave the Zearotts alone. They're no threat to you. In fact, you need to give up your position with the Council. You're a bad leader, and sometimes even a bad person."

Laura bit her lip. "Fine. I'm tired of this, anyway. Maybe I'll go work for Martin."

Everyone turned toward Mr. Jones. "Um...let's not get ahead of ourselves," he stammered.

"Has anyone talked to Mrs. Zearott?" Mercedes asked Jack, as they got David's belongings together. The nurses had already put him in a wheelchair and brought him down to the lobby.

"Yeah, Parshall called her right after everything happened. They both agreed that even though the crisis seems averted, Zoe still needs to keep a low profile. She's going to stay an Albone, but Mrs. Zearott and the other daughters are going to move to Gainesville to be close to her."

"I think she'll like that. Your brother and his family are nice people. Maybe they'll adopt the whole Zearott family."

Jack snorted. "The daughters would have to change their names to Lucy."

"You're kidding about that, right?"

"I hope so."

Herb and Yvonne were still recovering from their out-of-body experiences. However, Renna met David down in the lobby. She leaned over to hug him, but he was still too weak to hug her back. Not being able to move for so long had taken a toll on him.

"You're alright now. We won't let anything like that happen to you again."

He jerked his head back to get his longer-than-usual hair out of his eyes. "You can't promise that."

"Well, I can't, but I think my grandmother can. How crazy is that? She's like the Queen of the Soulpushers!"

"I heard. That lady is fierce. We need to invite her to Jacksonville more often."

Renna smiled. "Maybe sometime we can go visit her. It's been a long time since I've been out that way."

Parshall came up behind Renna and hugged her. "I'm going to accompany David back home and help him get used to being back in his body. Regina said she might stick around, but I told her I'm good. After all, I'm the new Council leader. I need to step up."

Renna smiled. "Congratulations! I think you'll bring about some good change."

Parshall spotted Mercedes and Jack getting off the elevator. She also saw Luisa in the gift shop and waved. The older woman returned the wave and went back to pretending to look at magazines.

Renna waved goodbye to them all, and went down the hallway toward the cafeteria, looking for brownie sundaes.

The Company

The CEO sat down at his computer Monday morning and opened up the shared drive. He expected to see the usual reports and graphs, but something else caught his eye.

There was a new image on the drive. He opened it up and what he saw made his heart skip a few beats. A picture of Regina Sheardon pushing a soul out of a living body. Most people would look at it and think she was doing a mime act, but he knew exactly what she was doing. He could see the glimmer of the spirit emerging.

He brought up Doug's social media account. The CEO remembered Doug telling him that he had set his phone to automatically publish images and videos.

The picture had already been shared 30,000 times. He wished he hadn't done that, because now everyone would know. However, they now had the ammunition they needed to go to the Board. Operation Soul Relocation would be back on.

About the Author

Lola Lariscy was born and raised in Savannah. As an act of defiance, she left Georgia at age 17 for somewhere greater. Yet somehow, she ended up in Alabama, where she took ten years to earn a Bachelor of Arts degree in English, which set her up perfectly for a decades-long career in customer service.

During this time Lola wrote short stories and a novella. Eventually she completed her first novel, *Trudie Lem: Spaceship Captain, Earth Detective*. After suffering days of no responses from potential literary agents, she took matters into her own hands. She edited, formatted and published the book herself.

Eleven years later she was ready to publish her second novel. She did not want to format it herself because she was tired and her head hurt.

This second book is what you're looking at right now.